HOPE JONES
SAVES THE WORLD

JOSH LACEY

ILLUSTRATED BY
BEATRIZ CASTRO

ANDERSEN PRESS

YOUR PLASTIC IS KILLING TURTLES!

First published in 2020 by
Andersen Press Limited
20 Vauxhall Bridge Road
London SW1V 2SA

www.andersenpress.co.uk

2 4 6 8 10 9 7 5 3 1

Photo of Nelson Mandela courtesy of *South Africa The Good News*

British Library Cataloguing in Publication Data available.

ISBN 978 1 78344 927 9

This book is printed on FSC accredited paper

Printed and bound in Great Britain by Clays Ltd, Elcograf S.p.A.

I'M GIVING UP PLASTIC TO SAVE OUR OCEANS!

TOGETHER WE'RE GOING TO SAVE THE WORLD!

Hello.

Welcome to my blog.

My name is Hope Jones.

I am ten years old.

I am going to save the world.

'How wonderful it is that nobody need wait a single moment before starting to improve the world.'
ANNE FRANK

'Unless someone like you cares a whole awful lot, Nothing is going to get better. It's not.'
DR SEUSS

'A defiant deed has greater value than innumerable thousands of words.'
Emmeline Pankhurst

'Remember to look up at the stars and not down at your feet. Try to make sense of what you see and wonder about what makes the universe exist. Be curious. And however difficult life may seem, there is always something you can do and succeed at. It matters that you don't just give up.'
STEPHEN HAWKING

'IT IS TIME TO REBEL.'
GRETA THUNBERG

'THE EARTH IS WHAT WE ALL HAVE IN COMMON.'
WENDELL BERRY

'Earth provides enough to satisfy every man's needs, but not every man's greed.'
MAHATMA GANDHI

MONDAY 30 DECEMBER

If you're wondering why I want to save the world, the answer is very simple. The world is in a mess.

You do know that, don't you?

If you don't, you just have to pick your nose.

Stick your finger up there and pull out a bogey.

What colour is it?

Mine are black.

Yes. Black.

From the pollution.

Look:

Sorry, I know that's gross. But you know what is even more gross? Having black bogeys. They should be green, right? Not black.

Perhaps you live on the top of a mountain or in the middle of the countryside, and the air is lovely and clean, and your bogeys are bright green.

But I live in the city. And mine are black, which is how I know the world is in a mess. Someone needs to save it.

Dad always says if you want to get something done, you have to do it yourself. So I'm going to.

I'll write here every day about saving the world. So please come back and see what I've said. You can't leave a comment, because Dad says the internet is full of nutters and he doesn't want me communicating with them.

I don't think any nutters will want to read my blog, but Dad said, 'You'd be surprised.' So the comments are switched off.

But if you send me an email, I will write back ASAP (unless you're a nutter).

My email is **hopejonessavestheworld@gmail.com**

You could even send me a picture of your bogeys.

Actually, please don't.

Bye for now!

See you tomorrow.

TUESDAY 31 DECEMBER

Hello!

It's me again. Hope.

You're probably wondering who I am. Sorry, I should have introduced myself properly, but I got distracted by all that stuff about bogeys. So today I'm going to tell you a bit more about myself.

My name is Hope Rose Jones.

I am ten years old.

My favourite colours are red and black.

My favourite foods are lasagna, black olives, and chocolate ice cream.

My worst fears are global warming and spiders.

I am not going to tell you where I live, because we did an internet safety class at school, and we were told never to reveal our actual addresses or phone numbers to strangers.

But I can tell you that I live with my mum and dad.

This is what they look like:

I have one brother and one sister. I'm in the middle, which is definitely the worst place to be. It's nice being the eldest, because you get to stay up late, and have more pocket money, and you have the biggest room. And it's nice being the youngest, because everyone says you're cute, and basically you get away with everything, and no one ever tells you off. But being in the middle is rubbish.

Unfortunately there's nothing I can do about it.

Anyway, this is my little brother Finn. He won't stay still, which is why you can only see the back of his head. He's always running around and shouting, but no one ever tells him off, because he's the youngest. Like I said, he gets away with everything.

This is my big sister Becca. She's sixteen. She's usually quite nice, but today she kicked me out of her room for being annoying, which wasn't exactly friendly.

I think she's just depressed because it's New Year's Eve and she's stuck at home with us.

She says she's the only sixteen-year-old on the planet who isn't going to a party tonight. Aunt Jess says Becca's got the rest of her life to go to parties and she should enjoy welcoming in the New Year with us.

Aunt Jess is very cool. She isn't going to a New Year's Eve party because she's just broken up with her evil boyfriend. I suppose he's now her evil ex-boyfriend. He's not really evil. But he dumped her in a horrid way. So she's not in the mood for parties, which is why she's babysitting tonight.

She's going to let us stay up till midnight as long as we go to bed without any fuss afterwards.

So now I've introduced you to my whole family. We also have two pets.

Here is our cat Poppadom.   This is our hamster Chutney.

Obviously Chutney and Poppadom won't help me save the world, but I hope the others will.

Today is the last day of the year.

The seconds are ticking down . . .

Till tomorrow . . .

The first day of the new year . . . When I'm going to start saving the world. I can't wait!

I've already made my resolution. Do you want to know what it is?

I'll tell you. Tomorrow.

I have to go now. We're making flapjacks with Aunt Jess.

See you next year!

WEDNESDAY 1 JANUARY

HAPPY! New! Year!

Today is a big day. I am going to start saving the world.

So here is my New Year's resolution: I am giving up plastic.

Do you want to know why? It's very simple. Plastic is making a mess of the whole world. Look at this:

I didn't actually take that picture. I've never been to Hawaii, although I definitely want to one day. It is the birthplace of surfing. I love surfing.

Anyway, like I said, I've never been there, but I found that photo on the internet. And it made me really sad. Look at all those bottles! Some of them floated all the way from Canada. Others came from Japan and China. There are even a couple from England.

Ten years ago that beach was a beautiful spotless sandy beach. The perfect place to go surfing. Or lay your eggs if you were a turtle or a seagull searching for somewhere nice and quiet to bring up your babies.

Now it's covered in plastic. You wouldn't want to surf there. Or bring up your babies. That lovely beach has been ruined. But it's not only beaches that have been messed up by plastic. It's also the lives of birds and animals.

Look at this:

Have you ever seen anything so horrible? That poor turtle!

At the end of last term we watched a documentary about the ocean. There were whales and walruses and dolphins and plankton and coral and all kinds of other amazing stuff. There was also this turtle who suffocated and died because she got a plastic balloon trapped in her tummy. It was the saddest thing I have ever seen. I couldn't stop thinking about that turtle. I used to love balloons. But not any more.

What if the balloon which suffocated that turtle was one of the plastic balloons from one of my birthday parties? Even if I hadn't killed that particular turtle, I might have been responsible for the death of a seagull or a jellyfish or some other ocean creature strangled or poisoned by a plastic balloon.

And it's not just plastic balloons that kill turtles. It's also plastic straws and plastic bottles and plastic bags and all sorts of plastic rubbish, floating in the ocean, poisoning the planet, and killing creatures everywhere.

1. More plastic has already been produced in the twenty-first century than during the whole of the twentieth century.

2. Less than a tenth of all plastic is recycled.

3. The tiniest pieces of plastic are called microplastics. They are now everywhere — in fish, in animals, in our food, in our bodies.

4. The average person eats a hundred microplastics in every meal.

5. Plastic kills at least a million birds every year.

6. Plastic kills at least a hundred thousand marine animals every year.

7. Two million plastic bags are used around the world every day.

8. Each one is used for an average of ten minutes, then thrown away.

I did some research. I discovered some horrible facts about plastic. They made me feel very depressed. And extremely guilty about all the plastic that I've used in my life. So I made a decision. My New Year's resolution is to never use plastic again.

No plastic bags. No plastic bottles. No plastic balloons.

No. More. Plastic.

The Jones Family's New Year's Resolutions

ME

I am giving up plastic.

MUM

Mum's resolution is running 5K at least three times per week, so she has bought herself some new trainers and new tracksuit bottoms and a new sports bra. She hasn't actually done any running yet, but it's only the first day of the year, so can everyone please give her a break.

DAD

Dad's resolution is giving up alcohol for January except in unforeseen circumstances. I asked him what 'unforeseen circumstances' are, but he said he didn't know, because they're unforeseen. I think he means having a bad day at work.

FINN

Finn's resolution is playing for Manchester United, which isn't exactly likely, but Mr Ilkley says it's good to have high aspirations.

Mr Ilkley is the coach of his team in the Junior Football League, and is a big fan of positive thinking. He says nothing is impossible if you set your mind to it.

I hope he's right, because it will be the first time in history that a seven-year-old has played for Manchester United.

BECCA

Becca has twelve resolutions written on her phone, but she won't let me see them, because they're strictly private. I think they must have something to do with finding a boyfriend. She's been wanting a boyfriend for ages, but a good man is hard to find. That's what Becca says, anyway.

POPPADOM

Obviously Poppadom doesn't have any resolutions, but I wish she would stop chasing birds, because the time that she caught a sparrow was traumatic for all concerned.

CHUTNEY

Obviously he doesn't have any resolutions either.

Hope Jones' Blog

Dear grown-ups,

I don't know if you're reading this. I don't know if any kids are, either. But if you are reading this, and you're a grown-up, I would like you to know one thing: you have made a mess of the world.

Yes, you. Grown-ups.

Not just you personally. But all the grown-ups throughout history. You have turned our world into an enormous horrible mess. Please clean it up!

You're probably wondering why I'm asking you to do this, rather than doing it myself, and the answer is very simple. Kids haven't messed up the world. We've just arrived.

We're looking around. Finding out what's new. How to walk. How to talk. How to tie our shoes. How to read and write. Our favourite foods. Our favourite colours. Our likes and dislikes.

But you . . . Grown-ups! You have messed up the world.

So please, please, please . . . Clean it up!

I know some of you do already. You clean up after yourselves. You recycle, re-use, and reduce your consumption.

But some of you don't. Take Mr Crabbe, for instance. He's our next-door neighbour. Today was rubbish day. Here are his recycling bins:

I thought he must have forgotten because of the holidays, so I knocked on his door to tell him, but he wasn't at all grateful. In fact, he told me to mind my own business.

I said, 'Don't you care about the planet?'

Mr Crabbe said when was the last time the planet had done anything for him? My mind boggled. I literally didn't know where to begin. Without the planet, there wouldn't be any metal to build that great big enormous car that he loves so much. There wouldn't be any rubber to make the tyres. There wouldn't be any bricks to build his house. There wouldn't be any food for him to eat. In fact, he wouldn't even exist.

Unfortunately I didn't get a chance to say any of this, because Mr Crabbe had already stormed back inside and shut the door in my face.

Mr Crabbe, if you're reading my blog, I hope you don't mind me saying this, but you really should do more recycling. Also, you should work on your people skills.

And if any other adults are reading this then, please, please, please, clean up your own mess!

Thank you!

Love from
Hope

Hope Jones' Blog

FRIDAY 3 JANUARY

Have you ever been to a supermarket? I bet you have. I have too. A million times. But today was the first day that I noticed what the supermarket sells more than anything.

Not food. No.

Obviously there was a lot of food for sale, but the supermarket was actually selling something which you didn't even have to pay for.

Plastic!

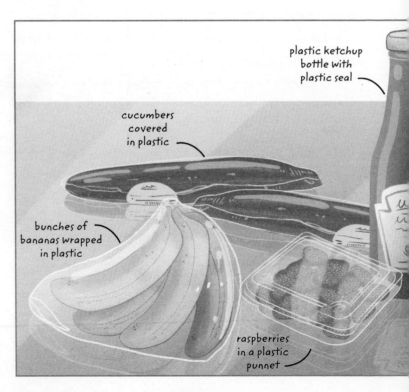

plastic ketchup bottle with plastic seal

cucumbers covered in plastic

bunches of bananas wrapped in plastic

raspberries in a plastic punnet

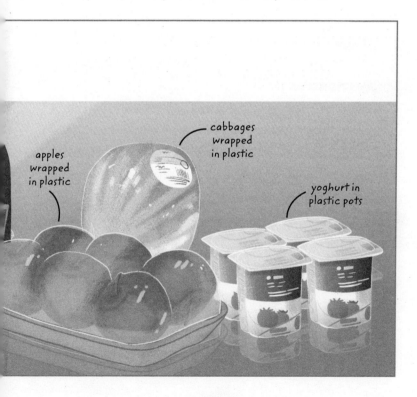

There was plastic literally everywhere. Plastic bottles. Plastic jars. Plastic cups. Plastic cartons. Plastic wrappers. Plastic bags.

Every time you buy something in the supermarket, it is literally covered in plastic. Which you don't have to pay for. And you probably don't even want. But you get it anyway.

The cucumbers are covered in plastic. The cabbages are wrapped in plastic. The yoghurt comes in plastic pots. The plastic ketchup bottle has a plastic seal under its plastic lid.

apples
wrapped
in plastic

cabbages
wrapped
in plastic

yoghurt in
plastic pots

Mum did her best. She tried not to buy any plastic. We put broccoli and onions and carrots straight in the trolley, rather than using plastic bags. We bought a glass bottle of ketchup instead of the plastic one. And obviously we took reusable linen bags instead of buying new plastic ones.

Did you know teabags are made with plastic? Mum was shocked to hear that. So she bought loose-leaf tea instead. She says it's nicer anyway, even though it's more of a hassle. The tea did actually come in a plastic bag inside their cardboard box, but we didn't find out till we got home. Which just shows how there is plastic everywhere in that supermarket, even when you can't see it immediately.

Anyway, like I said, we did our best. But even so, there must have been enough plastic in our trolley to murder an entire family of turtles. Mum and I had a fight about it. I wanted to take out everything which used plastic. She said then we'd be left with nothing to eat for the whole week.

You know what? She was right.

I felt terrible. My New Year's resolution was giving up plastic. But look at all the plastic in our trolley!

The toilet cleaner comes in a plastic bottle. The toilet paper is wrapped in plastic. So are the sausages. The milk comes in a plastic bottle. The cream comes in a plastic carton. There is plastic literally everywhere.

I talked to the woman at the checkout. Her name was Serena. She was very nice. But she wasn't much help. I asked Serena why there was so much plastic in her shop.

'Don't ask me,' Serena said. 'I just work here.'

I said, 'Then who should I ask?'

Serena wasn't really sure. 'You could talk to my manager.'

She had a look around, but there wasn't any sign of her manager. He must have been on a break. So Serena gave me the manager's name, and his email address, and suggested I should write a letter if I had any issues.

Serena was very interested in my New Year's resolution. She has six grandchildren, and she is worried about the world that they're going to grow up in. She said from now on she's going to try and use less plastic too. As soon as we got home, I wrote a letter to the branch manager. He hasn't replied yet. But I'll tell you as soon as he does.

FROM Hope Jones
TO Jeremy Schnitzel
DATE Friday 3 January
SUBJECT Plastic

Dear Mr Schnitzel

This morning I went to your supermarket and I was shocked by the amount of plastic.

Don't you know plastic is bad for the environment? For instance, if someone drops a plastic bag in the ocean, it will float around for hundreds of years. During that time, it is very likely to cause trouble for a turtle, a seagull, a seal, a walrus, or some other bird, fish, or mammal.

Plastic bags aren't the only problem. Plastic bottles are just as bad. So are plastic cartons and plastic wrappers.

Your shop is full of plastic. But it really doesn't have to be. For instance, you really don't need a plastic bag just to wrap up a couple of apples or some tomatoes.

I'm sure you don't want to destroy the planet. So please can you use less plastic in your shop?

Thank you!

Yours sincerely

Hope Jones

SATURDAY 4 JANUARY

I give up!

I can't do this any more!

There is so much plastic everywhere!

Don't worry. I'm not really giving up. It's only the fourth day of the year and stopping my resolution now would be pathetic. Mum has been jogging, and Dad still hasn't touched a drop since New Year's Eve, and I'm definitely not giving up before either of them. No way! Because the planet needs me.

But there is just so much plastic everywhere!

Reduce. Re-use. Recycle. That's what I keep telling myself.

But it's so difficult! It is almost impossible.

For instance, I just looked under the sink. I couldn't believe the amount of plastic. There were plastic bags, and plastic wrappers, and seven plastic cartons, which someone had kept, although I don't know what for. There was a spare plastic washing-up brush, and a plastic packet full of plastic sponges, and two plastic washing-up liquid bottles, and a roll of plastic rubbish bags, and a plastic bag full of other plastic bags, and a plastic bag filled with twenty dishwasher tablets which were individually wrapped in plastic – what a waste!

Don't get me started on the fridge.

After my experiences under the sink, I was feeling terrible. Dad said a walk in the park would cheer us up. He was right. It did. Especially when we flew the new kite that Finn got for Christmas.

On the way home, we stopped in a café for a special treat. That was a mistake. A big mistake.

I had brought my reusable water bottle and a Tupperware box for snacks, so I didn't actually need anything, but the others weren't so well prepared. Finn wanted a hot chocolate, which came in a plastic cup. He also had a small packet of ginger biscuits, which came in a plastic wrapping. Becca had a smoothie in a plastic bottle. Mum and Dad had forgotten the reusable coffee cup, which I gave them for Christmas, so they both used plastic cups.

Even the plastic spoons were wrapped in plastic!

I talked to the woman behind the counter. She was really nice, but she said she couldn't help. She said the owner had just popped out, but I could leave him a note or write him a message. She gave me his email address.

I wrote to him as soon as we got home. I copied and pasted some of the message from my email to Mr Schnitzel, because Dad said it would be more efficient, and no one would ever know. I hope he's right.

FROM Hope Jones
TO Brendan Corrigan
DATE Saturday 4 January
SUBJECT Plastic

Dear Mr Corrigan

This morning I went to your café.

I love Flat White. It's the nicest café ever.

I don't actually like flat whites. Or any other coffees. But the hot chocolates are deeeee-licious. Especially the ones with extra whipped cream and a sprinkling of marshmallows. My dad loves your coffee too. And the cakes are yummy. I would like to go to your café every day.

But there's just one problem. You use so much plastic! The smoothies. The flapjacks. Even the plastic spoons. They're all wrapped in plastic!

Don't you know plastic is bad for the environment? For instance, if someone drops a plastic bag in the ocean, it will float around for hundreds of years. During that time, it is very likely to cause trouble for a turtle, a seagull, a seal, a walrus, or some other bird, fish, or mammal.

Plastic bags aren't the only problem. Plastic bottles are just as bad. So are plastic cartons and plastic wrappers. Your café is full of plastic. But it really doesn't have to be. You really don't need to wrap up your plastic spoons in their own plastic wrapping. You could use metal spoons instead. You could use reusable cups instead of plastic ones. You could make your own smoothies instead of selling ones in plastic bottles. They would be much nicer. And better for your customers.

I'm sure you don't want to destroy the planet. So please can you use less plastic in your café?

Thank you!

Yours sincerely

Hope Jones

Mr Corrigan hasn't replied yet. Mr Schnitzel hasn't replied either. I am worried he didn't get my email.

I asked Mum if we could go to the supermarket again and have a word with him. She said all we need is bread and milk, and we can get that round the corner.

When we went to Mr Ghosh to buy bread and milk, we took our own bag, but we still ended up buying a lot of useless plastic. The bread came in a plastic bag. The milk came in a plastic bottle. Even the bran flakes came in a plastic bag inside the cardboard box.

I asked Mum not to buy any of them, but she said, 'Then what will you have for breakfast tomorrow morning?' I'd be happy with a tangerine and some leftover flapjack, but apparently that's not enough for the others. They need toast and cereal.

I asked Mum not to buy any frozen peas either, or rice, or crisps, because they all came in plastic packaging, but she said she couldn't turn her entire life around just because of my New Year's resolution. I don't see why not. I know it's inconvenient. But wouldn't it be even more inconvenient if we didn't have a planet to live on?

In the old days, when Mum and Dad were kids, people used glass bottles for milk. So they could be re-used and recycled. I wish they hadn't changed to plastic. Dad says you can still get milk in glass bottles, but they are five times the price, and unfortunately he's not made of money. He said I'm welcome to give up milk and have water with my bran flakes instead if I'm so worried.

I reminded him that I don't eat bran flakes any more, because they come in a plastic bag inside the cardboard box. I'm going to have porridge instead.

'Fine,' Dad said. 'You don't need milk with that.'

I was still feeling bad about the bread, the milk, the frozen peas, the rice, the crisps, and the olives. Then things got even worse. We had a competition to build Lego towers.

Becca said she's too old for silly competitions, not to mention Lego, so it was just me, Finn, and Dad.

Obviously Dad's a lot older than Becca, but he says nothing would make him happier than beating his children in a Lego-tower-building competition.

Mine would have been the tallest, but Finn knocked it down with his Frisbee just as I was applying the finishing touches.

Finn said it was a mistake, but I wasn't born yesterday. I was just about to demand a re-match when Becca said, 'Have you ever noticed what Lego is made of?'

I hadn't. But she's absolutely right. Plastic.

Then she said, 'What do you think that's made of?'

She was pointing at my tablet.

I said, 'Glass.'

'And?'

'Metal.'

'And something else too,' Becca said.

She was right about that too.

There is plastic everywhere.

Dad came to find me.

He said, 'What's wrong, pumpkin?'

I hate it when he calls me that. I'm not three years old. I said, 'Nothing.'

He said, 'Then why are you crying?'

I could have lied. Or asked him to go away. But in the end, I told the truth. I was crying because I felt terrible about the world and plastic and my resolution and how impossible everything is.

I don't want to give up my tablet. It's my best Christmas present ever. But it's made of plastic! So what am I supposed to do?

Dad said we're all confronted by difficult choices and we just have to try our hardest and do our best.

'Come on,' he said. 'Let's go and look on the internet. I bet we can find something to cheer us up.'

I thought he meant silly videos, but actually he meant the price of milk. He has looked up the price of milk in glass bottles. It isn't actually five times the price. It's only two and a half times. He said we could afford that, especially if we're all very careful and make sure we don't use more than we need. So he's ordered it from next Tuesday.

At least we're not going to use any more plastic milk cartons. It's a good start. That's what Dad thinks. And I suppose he's right.

After we'd ordered the milk, we researched alternatives for the other plastic products in our house. We found lots. It isn't going to be easy. In fact it will be hard work. But I don't care. We'll be making the world a better place.

Welcome . . .

To a very special place . . .

Our bathroom!

Sometimes this special place is full of danger . . . You might be attacked by a bad smell . . . Or an angry teenager who needs some private time. If you're really unlucky, you might even find an enormous terrifying spider which has crawled out of the plughole. But today we have the bathroom to ourselves. And we can go on a hunt for plastic.

Let's start with the big things:

Yes. I'm sorry to say they're all made of plastic. The bath. The toilet seat. The shower curtain. All plastic. The taps might be metal, but they have plastic fittings. The light is plastic too. Even the clips on the mirror are made of plastic. But that's not everything. Look at this:

That's just Becca's shelf. Mum has almost as much. And this is all plastic too:

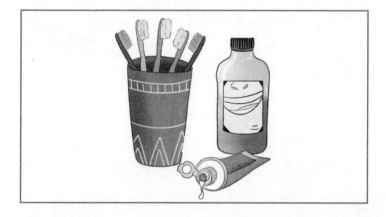

There is plastic literally everywhere in our bathroom. The toilet cleaner comes in a plastic bottle. The toilet brush is made of plastic. The toilet paper isn't plastic. But it comes in a plastic wrapper. The soap isn't plastic either. But it comes in a plastic dispenser. Some of these plastic things can be reused. Others can be recycled. But most of them aren't. Most of them just get thrown away and replaced.

Or they would have done, anyway. Until now. Change is coming. Come back in a week and there won't be any plastic in this bathroom!

(Apart from the bath. And the shower curtain. And the toilet seat.)

THINGS TO DO

- Buy toilet paper which isn't wrapped in plastic.

- Buy old-fashioned soap.

- Make toilet cleaner from vinegar, lemon, and baking soda.

- Replace the plastic toilet brush with a wooden one.

- Buy bamboo toothbrushes.

- Persuade Becca to use reusable and recyclable packaging for shampoo, tampons, make-up, shower gel, mascara, etc. Mum too.

- Dad is going to buy an old-fashioned razor so he doesn't have to throw away any more plastic razors.

- Find a way to get toothpaste which isn't in a plastic tube????

SUNDAY 5 JANUARY

This morning, I had porridge made with water instead of milk. It wasn't very nice. But at least I didn't use any plastic. I can't wait till the new milk bottles start arriving.

After breakfast, Dad and I went on the internet. We bought toilet roll that is delivered to your house in a cardboard box. Dad ordered forty-eight rolls, which should be enough to keep us going. He ordered some bars of soap too. We won't be using any more plastic soap dispensers.

I have been researching shampoo and shower gel alternatives. I'm trying to persuade Becca to change her habits. She isn't very enthusiastic about it. In fact, when I suggested she should use reusable and recyclable packaging for her shampoo, tampons, make-up, and shower gel, she said, 'Not in a million years.' But I'm sure she'll change her mind soon.

We cleaned our toilet with environmentally friendly ingredients. Mum was delighted. She hates cleaning the toilet. I don't know why. I thought it was fun.

HOW TO CLEAN THE TOILET
WITH HOMEMADE TOILET CLEANER

- Sprinkle baking soda into the toilet.

- Leave for five minutes. Scrub well.

- Pour vinegar into the toilet. Scrub again.

- Pour in a few drops of lavender oil to make it smell nice. And you're done!

- Most toilet cleaner includes bleach and hydrochloric acid, which are extremely poisonous to us and to the environment. Also, most toilet cleaners come in plastic bottles. So this homemade toilet cleaner is better in every way.

After all that, I was feeling quite pleased with myself.
Then I got an email from Mr Corrigan and I felt even better.

FROM Brendan Corrigan
TO Hope Jones
DATE Sunday 5 January
SUBJECT Re: Plastic

Hey Hope

Thanks for your message. I absolutely agree about plastic.
And saving the world. In fact I've been trying to think of
ways to make my café more eco-friendly. You've given me
a few good ideas. I'm going to start making some changes.
Right now.

Next time you're passing, come and say hi.

Respect.

Brendan

I was feeling very pleased about the toilet paper, the glass milk bottles, the soap, and Mr Corrigan's email.

Then it was lunchtime. And everything went wrong. Mum made a roast. We had roast chicken (which came in plastic packaging) and roast potatoes (which came in a plastic bag) and frozen peas (which came in a plastic bag) followed by apricot tart (which came in a plastic wrapper inside a cardboard box) and a choice of cream (plastic carton) or vanilla ice cream (plastic tub).

Mum said she was very sorry about all the plastic, but she can't change the world all alone, particularly when she's got three children to feed, not to mention her job, and her course, which starts again next week.

Finn said if I wasn't having pudding, then could he have cream *and* ice cream, rather than either/or, which shows how much he cares about the planet.

I spent a long time wondering what to do. Should I just have tangerines and flapjack for lunch, therefore not using any plastic?

Or should I have roast chicken and roast potatoes and frozen peas and apricot tart and either cream or ice cream, therefore using a lot of plastic, but plastic that would have been used anyway by the rest of my family?

I know eating only tangerines and flapjack was the right thing to do. But I had the nice lunch.

I just couldn't resist. It smelled so delicious. And all that worrying made me really hungry.

Now I feel bad. I'm not the solution. I'm part of the problem.

Mum thinks I should give up **hopejonessavestheworld.com**. She says a ten-year-old girl can't possibly save the world on her own, and it's the last few days of the holidays, so why don't I relax and enjoy myself, rather than worrying all the time?

But I can't. I do feel worried all the time.

I'm worried about the future.

I'm worried about the oceans.

I'm worried about the planet.

I'm worried about plastic.

I can't relax when the world is in such a mess!

So I've been thinking about more ways to save the planet and stop using plastic. I've done the kitchen. And the bathroom.

What next?

PETS HATE PLASTIC!

Do you use a plastic bag for your dog's poop?
Does your cat do its business in a plastic tray?
Do you buy pet food in plastic pouches?

Yes? Well, it's time to stop.

- Don't pick up their poop in a plastic bag!
  Scoop it up with a shovel instead. Or use
  a biodegradable bag.

- When you're buying pet food, buy in bulk! And
  take your own bag to the shop. Then you don't
  need any plastic.

- Your pets don't need plastic toys! Instead you
  can buy pet toys made from rope or cotton or
  recycled rubber.

- Hamster straw can go straight on the compost.
  So no need for plastic rubbish bags. (Don't do
  this with dog poo or cat litter.)

Hope Jones' Blog

Do you know about Greenham Common?

I didn't. Until today. But now I do. And you know what? It's given me a brilliant idea. I'll tell you all about it. But first I've got to tell you about Greenham Common.

But before I tell you about Greenham Common, I need to tell you about my friend Harry's mum's auntie. I've never actually met her, but I heard all about her today when I went round to Harry's house. To be honest I wasn't really in the mood for seeing anyone, because of still not getting a reply from Mr Schnitzel, but Mum said we'd arranged it weeks ago, so it would be rude not to go.

I have been best friends with Harry Murakami for about a year. Before that, my best friend was Zoe Madrigal, but she moved away. Harry isn't like me. In fact, we're extremely different. But that's why we're such good friends. We can always find something to talk about.

Harry is actually the one who made this blog for me. He is only ten years old, but he knows everything about computers. He owns six of them. Yes, six! He didn't buy any. One came from his dad's office. He found another on a skip and brought it back to life. He's like that. He's a genius with computers. He's going to be a famous scientist when he grows up.

Harry has a very interesting family. His dad is from Japan, and his mum is from Bedford, which means they are culturally mixed.

He has been to Tokyo three times to visit his grandparents. He would like to go there more often, but the price of the flights is astronomical.

Harry shares my feelings about the state of the world. He says it's a mess too. But he's not worried about it like I am. He says I've got to stop being pessimistic and start enjoying life a bit more. He says I shouldn't worry so much, because scientists can do anything, and they're going to save the world.

When he's older, he will invent a machine to protect the turtles, the dolphins, the walruses, and anything else which might otherwise get murdered by plastic. He's not exactly sure how the machine will work, but somehow it will suck all the plastic out of the ocean and turn it into something useful.

I just hope there are some creatures left in the ocean by the time he grows up.

Harry doesn't agree with my New Year's resolution. Harry said, 'What about the plastic chairs at school? Are you going to sit on the floor? Or stand up all day?'

I didn't know how to answer that.

Harry said, 'What about computers? They're made of plastic. Do you want me to stop using them?'

I didn't know how to answer that either.

Harry said, 'Doctors use plastic all the time. What about all the people whose lives they save? Do you want those people to die?'

Obviously I don't.

It's the silly pointless plastic that I'm worried about. The plastic that you don't actually need at all.

Plastic balloons. Plastic water bottles. Plastic straws. Plastic bags. Plastic knives and plastic forks and plastic spoons. That plastic isn't saving people's lives. But it is killing turtles and seagulls and walruses and dolphins.

Harry's mum wanted to know what we were talking about. So we told her. Harry's mum said, 'You're as bad as my auntie.'

I said, 'What's wrong with your auntie?'

Harry's mum said, 'She spent most of the 1980s camped outside Greenham Common.'

We had never heard of Greenham Common, but Harry's mum

told us all about it and showed us some pictures on the internet. Apparently the Americans wanted to keep some of their bombs in Britain, but some British women said, no thanks, because what if the bombs went off by mistake and blew us all up?

The British government agreed with the Americans, which made the British women really upset. Then they had a brilliant idea. Lots of them went and protested outside the airfield where the Americans were keeping their bombs. They chained themselves to the fences and sang songs and painted banners and put up tents and built a camp, because they wanted to make the country safe.

It took nineteen years for the British women to win the battle, but in the end, the Americans took their bombs home again.

At first I didn't believe the British women were really camped outside Greenham Common for nineteen years, but it's true.

They were. Not the same ones all the time. But some. And Harry's mum's auntie was one of them.

I felt very guilty. I had wanted to give up saving the world after less than a week. Those women carried on for nineteen years!

Next time Harry's mum's auntie comes to stay with the Murakamis, they're going to invite me round. I can't wait to meet her. Harry says she's really nice. When I get to meet her, I want to say thank you in person. Because while I was looking at the pictures, I got my brilliant idea.

I literally jumped up in the air and shouted 'YES!'

Harry put his hands over his ears. He doesn't like loud noises.

His mum said, 'Blimey, you really are as mad as my auntie.'

I apologised to both of them. But I couldn't help myself. I was just too excited. I knew my idea was brilliant.

As soon as I got home, I asked Mum if she had any old sheets. She said only the one which Dad used to cover the floor when he painted Finn's room. It was covered in dusts and flecks of blue paint, but that doesn't matter.

I found two bamboo sticks in the garden. Then I painted some words on the sheet and tied it to the bamboo sticks and made a banner.

The women at Greenham Common pitched their tents by the main gates and stayed there for nineteen years.

Mum and Dad won't let me pitch my tent outside the supermarket. But Mum has agreed to take me and my banner there tomorrow, so I can protest while she does the shopping.

I can't wait.

I'm so excited.

I'm never going to sleep tonight.

TUESDAY 7 JANUARY

Wow. Today was A-Mazing. I think it might have been the most amazing day of my life.

This morning, I set my alarm for 6.30am.

When Dad got up, I was already working on my banner. He said, 'I thought you were meant to be on holiday.'

'I am,' I said.

'So why aren't you in bed?'

'I'm busy.'

'Me too,' Dad said. 'Unfortunately.'

Dad works for local government, which means he spends all day in meetings with people who love the sound of their own voices.

Dad said, 'Is this about your protest?'

I said It was.

Dad said, 'I hope you're not intending to go protesting at seven o'clock in the morning.'

I said I wasn't intending to go anywhere till Mum got up, but I had to finish my banner. I told him I was going protesting later and he was very welcome to come too.

'I wish,' said Dad. 'Unfortunately some of us have to earn a living.'

When he went to work, he called me to have a look at something outside the front door. It was our first delivery.

54

They're going to arrive every Tuesday, Thursday, and Saturday. After we've finished the bottle, we put it outside for the milkman to take away and use again.

No more plastic bottles!

The others didn't get up for ages. But when they finally did, we went to the supermarket.

Becca refused to come with us. She said the whole idea was totally embarrassing and what if someone saw her?

I explained that the whole point was people seeing us, but she wouldn't change her mind. She just wanted to stay at home and play on her phone. So it was just me, Mum, and Finn standing outside the supermarket with my banner. Finn held one stick and I held the other.

At the beginning, we were all alone, and people were giving us funny looks. But things changed quickly.

The first person to talk to us was Mrs Ribblethwaite, who lives down the road. She said she was sorry her generation had left the world in such a mess, and she wanted to apologise to young people like me, and she hoped we would be able to undo all the damage, and make things better for the generations who come after us. I hope so too.

Mrs Ribblethwaite had only been going to the supermarket for a loaf of bread. After talking to us, she went to the bakery instead, because they put their bread in paper bags rather than plastic.

Lots of other people came to talk to us. They asked questions. They wanted to know about the turtles. They told us what they thought.

Some were quite rude. A boy laughed at me. Two girls shouted something nasty, which I'm not going to put here.

But most people were very friendly. A nice man told me about the war in Iraq. He went on a march with a banner just like mine. He said it's easy to be cynical and defeatist, but you still have to try.

Once Mum had explained what cynical and defeatist mean, I knew I didn't want to be them either. Especially not on my first day of protesting.

Mrs Ribblethwaite came back from the bakery with her bread and two extra paper bags, one each for me and Finn. Inside there were gingerbread men to keep our strength up, which was really very thoughtful of her. I was beginning to feel a bit tired.

Mrs Ribblethwaite stayed with us while Mum went into the supermarket to buy some basics. I reminded Mum not to buy any plastic. She promised not to.

Mrs Ribblethwaite didn't want to hold the banner. But she stood beside me and Finn, chatting to us, while we carried on protesting.

Mum had only been gone for a couple of minutes when this man came to meet us:

Can you guess who he is?

I'll tell you.

Mr Schnitzel!

At first I didn't know he was Mr Schnitzel, because I had only written him an email, so I had no idea what he looked like. I had noticed him staring at me, but I thought he was just interested in the banner.

Then he walked up to us. He said, 'Hello, my name is Jeremy Schnitzel, and I'm the manager of this store. Can I help you with anything?'

I said, 'Did you get my email?'

He said which email.

I said the one about the turtles.

He said he didn't know anything about any turtles, but could I take my protest somewhere else.

'Like where?' I said.

He said he didn't care as long as it wasn't in front of his shop, because I was putting off his customers.

I said I was sorry, but his customers needed to know about

the turtles, and so did he, and I wish he had read my email.

Mr Schnitzel said he was sorry he hadn't seen it, but he gets several hundred emails every day, and could I have a bit of understanding for his predicament. He said please could I move my protest elsewhere, because I was causing significant disruption to his customers.

I said lots of his customers agreed with me about the plastic and why couldn't he listen to them and use less in his shop.

He said decisions like that are outside his remit and he was just trying to do his job.

I said does his job include murdering turtles?

He said that was ridiculous and couldn't I please just stand a bit further away from the entrance to his store.

I refused. I also warned him that I would be coming back here to protest until he stopped using so much plastic in his shop. And I'd be here, every day, till he did.

He gave a big sigh. Then he said, 'Can't you try to see things from my point of view?'

I said, 'Can't you try to see things from the turtles' point of view?'

He said he didn't want to escalate the situation, but I was leaving him no choice.

I said fine.

While we were talking, two police officers came to have a look at my sign. Mr Schnitzel asked them to move me away. I felt quite nervous, but the police said I wasn't doing anything wrong. It was very good to know the law is on my side.

Suddenly Mum arrived. She had seen us through the window. She wanted to know what was going on.

'Are these your children?' said Mr Schnitzel.

When Mum said yes, Mr Schnitzel said we'd been causing a disturbance and upsetting customers who wanted to come to his shop. Which wasn't actually true. I tried to say so, but he wouldn't listen. It was like I wasn't there. He just talked to Mum. He told her that she shouldn't let her children behave so badly, and if she were a responsible parent, she wouldn't have left us outside the supermarket, unsupervised.

Mum didn't like him saying that. She told him that we were holding a peaceful protest, which was entirely within our rights as citizens, and she was very proud of us for caring about the environment. Then she said, 'I wish your store cared a bit more about the environment.'

'I do care about the environment,' Mr Schnitzel said. 'But I also care about my customers, and I don't want them to be disturbed while they're trying to do their shopping at my store.'

'My children aren't disturbing anyone,' Mum said. 'They're just holding a peaceful protest.'

'Couldn't they do it somewhere else?' Mr Schnitzel said.

'We have to do it here,' I said. 'You're the one using too much plastic!'

'Please don't shout at me,' Mr Schnitzel said.

Which was very unfair, because I hadn't.

Mum said, 'She wasn't shouting at you. She was just making her point. Which she has a perfect right to do.'

Mr Schnitzel must have realised that he was never going to win an argument with my mum, because he said he had to go back inside to deal with a spillage in aisle twenty-one.

When he had gone, Mum said, 'Who does he think he is?'

'The branch manager,' said Finn.

We all agreed that Mr Schnitzel needs to work on his people skills.

The two policewomen reassured me that we do have a perfect right to protest outside the supermarket, although they thought it would be best to go home at night, rather than staying in a tent outside the entrance like the women at Greenham Common.

When I got back home, I repainted my banner and decorated it with ribbons and glitter.

I know you shouldn't boast, but it looks absolutely amazing. Even Becca says so, and she has strong views on art and design.

I'm going to take it back to the supermarket tomorrow and do some more protesting.

And the day after.

And the day after that.

And the day after that.

And the day after that.

Until Mr Schnitzel removes all the plastic from his supermarket.

WEDNESDAY 8 JANUARY

Today was the last day of the holidays, so we had to go shopping. Finn insisted on buying a football shirt. I don't know how he persuaded Mum to get it for him. He's got so many already.

I got some new socks. And a cool T-shirt.

Our feet keep growing, so we both needed new school shoes and new plimsolls.

The woman in the shoe shop wanted to put my shoes in a plastic bag, but I said, no, thank you very much, I'd rather save the planet. Instead I bought a backpack with my Christmas money and put the shoes in there.

I ended up having a very interesting conversation with Cheryl, who runs the shoe shop. I told her about protesting outside the supermarket, and she said please don't protest outside her shop, because business is bad enough already.

I said I wouldn't if she stopped using plastic, and she said she would see what she can do, which usually means no, but I think Cheryl might actually mean yes. She said she would like her shoe shop to be plastic free, but it's very difficult. Apparently almost all shoes have some plastic in them, even if it's just the soles or the eyelets for the laces, but she's doing her best to cut down as much as possible. She's also going to start using cotton bags instead of plastic ones. From now on, I'm going to tell all my friends to buy their school shoes from her shop.

We went out for pizza for lunch. So we didn't get to the supermarket till this afternoon. Becca came too. She said she had to do some shopping, but I think she really wanted to know what I was doing. Mum had told her about the police officers and Mrs Ribblethwaite and Mr Schnitzel. Becca was really interested. Maybe she doesn't think I'm so annoying after all.

When we got there, Finn and I held up the sign. It looks even better with all the glitter. Finn got bored after about ten minutes. He had brought his football, although I asked him not to, and he tried to play keepy-uppy at the same time as holding the sign, which made the letters wobble so much no one would have been able to read the words.

Becca agreed to hold the sign instead. She said she'd drop it if she saw anyone from school. Luckily she didn't.

Mrs Goldstein came to say hello. When I told her about the turtles, she said, 'More power to your elbow!'

I'm not exactly sure what that meant. I asked Becca, but she said, 'If you don't know, I'm not going to tell you.' Which means she didn't know either.

Becca spent a long time talking to a girl called Sparkle about the positives and negatives of getting a nose ring.

Sparkle is a vegan. She told me that eating meat is the single biggest contributor to global warming, and if I'm really serious about saving the planet, I should become vegan too. She's going to lend me a book about it.

Sparkle had a friend called Tariq, who was really interested in the turtles.

He said previous generations have made a mess of the world, and it's our responsibility to make things right. I completely agree.

Tariq took our photo. Becca gave him her number so he could send it to us. He asked our permission to post it on social media too. We both said yes.

Tariq put these pictures on all his social media. He says the response has been amazing. Apparently his friends think I'm inspiring.

tariq

YOUR PLASTIC IS KILLING TURTLES

SPECIAL OFFERS

♡ **21 likes**

tariq Today I met these brilliant people who are protesting against the over-use of plastic at our local supermarket **#changetheworld #savetheplanet #girlpower #hopejonessavestheworld**

Could you put it on all your social media too? Please share it with all your friends and contacts. Because I want to spread my message as far and wide as possible.

Mr Schnitzel is just one branch manager in one supermarket. If he removed the plastic from his store, that would make a big difference. But imagine if every branch manager in every supermarket removed the plastic from their stores.

Think what a difference that would make!

tariq Change is coming! #dumpplastic #plasticboycott #changetheworld
#zerowaste #recycle #greenliving #savetheplanet #girlpower #handsoffourplanet
#wearethefuture #hopejonessavestheworld

Hope Jones' Blog

THURSDAY 9 JANUARY

Look at this!

Do you know what they are?

I'll tell you. They're Mr Crabbe's recycling boxes. As you can see, they're completely empty again.

While I was taking the picture, Mr Crabbe opened his front door and started shouting at me. I didn't mind. Sticks and stones. I said so to Mr Crabbe. He just shouted back even louder. He yelled at me that it's a crime to photograph other people's private property and he was going to report me to the council.

Fine. I'll report him first. For not recycling.

I told him that. I also told him what I think of his lack of recycling. I gave him some facts and figures about pollution and global warming. I would have told him a lot more, but Mum called me inside for breakfast.

'You've got school today,' she said. 'You don't want to be late on the first day, do you?'

I don't care if I'm late. I don't even want to go to school. Saving the world is a lot more important. That's what I think, anyway, but Mum doesn't agree.

I have been at school all day, and I have to tell you something. I am shocked. Shocked! Because of the plastic.

Our teacher Miss Brockenhurst handed out plastic folders for everyone at the beginning of the day.

Then she put plastic pens on the tables. In plastic pen pots. Most people have plastic pencil cases.

Seven children in my class don't even have their own water bottles, so they drink out of plastic water bottles. Their mums and dads buy them new ones every day. It must have been the same last term, but I didn't even notice then. Now I can't think about anything else. I counted up the number of school days in this term. There are fifty-nine. So each kid who buys a new water bottle every day will use fifty-nine plastic water bottles between today and the last day of term. That is a lot of water bottles. If I had enough pocket money, I'd buy them each a reusable water bottle myself.

At lunch the kitchen gave us plastic knives and plastic forks. At the end of lunch, they put all the plastic knives and plastic forks straight into the bin. They didn't even recycle them!

I felt very upset. And very annoyed. I talked to Mr Khan about it. He's the head. He said he appreciated my concern. He agreed that it would be better to have metal cutlery that could be washed and used again rather than plastic cutlery which has to be thrown away. He said he'll see what can be done.

I hope he will.

Jemima Higginbotham went to Madagascar for her Christmas holidays. She swam with sea turtles and saw lemurs and fed monkeys and bought cowrie shell necklaces for her seven best friends. (Obviously I'm not one of them.)

When we stood next to one another in PE, she said to me, 'What did you do in the holidays?'

I said, 'Not much.'

She said, 'That's sad.'

Somehow she said those words in a way which managed to really annoy me. I don't know how she does it.

I said, 'Did you think about the environmental impact of flying all the way to Madagascar and back again?'

She said, 'Not really.'

I said perhaps she should have.

She said, 'To be honest, I was too busy thinking about the lemurs. But you'll be glad to hear I took my reusable water bottle on the flight. So I did my bit for the planet.'

She does have a very nice reusable water bottle. It's stainless steel with a bamboo lid. I would like one myself, but they're very expensive. Maybe I'll ask Mum and Dad to give me one for my next birthday.

After school, we couldn't go to the supermarket, because Finn had football practice. I would have liked to protest on my own, but Mum wouldn't let me. Instead I had to stand by the goal and read my book while Finn was playing football, which is always quite boring.

As a special treat, Mum gave us crisps for a snack. She said it was the first day of term so we deserved it. But I couldn't eat them. The packet was made of plastic.

Finn didn't eat his either. I said he should do what he wanted.

He needed the energy for football practice. He said he was doing what he wanted, and he didn't want to eat those crisps if the bag couldn't be recycled. I told him he was the best brother in the world. For once I was glad he's always copying me.

So I didn't read my book during his football. Instead I shouted his name to encourage him and clapped every time he touched the ball. Then he scored a goal! It was actually quite exciting. Maybe he really will play for Manchester United one day.

FRIDAY 10 JANUARY

I will tell you one thing that I have learnt about changing the world. It's really quite tiring. Luckily I have a lot of energy. I know some ten year olds just want to watch TV or play games when they get home after school, but I'm not like that. I'm too energetic.

As soon as I got home, I wanted to go straight out again and do another protest at the supermarket. I didn't want Mr Schnitzel to think I've given up.

Mum said she was too busy to go today, and I'm not allowed out on my own. But she did say I could go with Becca, if Becca would agree to take me.

Becca didn't come back from netball club till ten past five. I asked if she would take me protesting, and she said, 'Give me a chance to sit down.'

In the end, she didn't just sit down. She also had a cup of tea, a glass of water, two apples, three chocolate biscuits, and the last piece of flapjack. Apparently netball gives you an appetite. But I'm not complaining, because when she'd finished her snack, she took me and Finn to the supermarket.

I think she was hoping to see Sparkle and Tariq again, but they weren't there.

We did meet some other interesting people.

One old lady said I was an example to us all.

I had a long conversation with a man called Luciano, who is visiting from Italy. I told him about the turtle which was suffocated

74

by a balloon, and he asked if I had ever swum with dolphins?

I said I haven't.

He said swimming with dolphins was the best thing he's done in his entire life and I should try it sometime.

I have added it to my bucket list.

HOPE'S BUCKET LIST

- See the Eiffel Tower
- Get a puppy
- Go to university
- Go surfing in Hawaii
- Learn how to make lasagna
- Climb Mount Everest
- Swim with dolphins

Luciano was drinking from a plastic bottle of water, which he had just bought in the supermarket. I said to him: 'Do you know three billion litres of bottled water are sold in the UK every year?'

He said he didn't know that.

I said to him: 'Can you imagine how many plastic bottles that is?'

He said probably a lot.

I said, 'It is a lot. And the water in those bottles isn't any cleaner or nicer than the water from the tap. In fact, it's probably dirtier. And tastes just the same. But the plastic bottles will last for hundreds of years. They'll float around the ocean. Maybe they'll end up on a beach. Or maybe they'll be eaten by a dolphin, and get stuck in its throat, and suffocate it.'

He said he'd never really thought about that, and he's going to buy a refillable water bottle, and never buy another plastic water bottle in his entire life. Instead he will always drink tap water.

After Luciano had gone, some of Becca's friends came past. She tried to hide behind the banner, but they spotted her straightaway.

I don't know why she was so embarrassed. Her friends all love turtles. They came and stood behind the banner. I heard one of them say to Becca, 'Your sister is really cool.'

'She's all right,' Becca said.

That might be the nicest thing she's ever said about me.

We all stood around the banner, shouting at the top of our voices. 'Save the turtles! Don't buy plastic! Save the turtles! Don't buy plastic!'

I could see Mr Schnitzel standing in the fresh vegetable section and staring at us through the window. I waved at him, but he pretended not to notice.

On the way home we stopped at Flat White to meet Mr Corrigan, but he wasn't there. He'd gone home for the day. The woman behind the counter said come back another day. She also said, 'Oh, you're Hope! He's been talking about you. He can't wait to meet you.'

I can't wait to meet him either.

Hope Jones' Blog

SATURDAY 11 JANUARY

Mr Schnitzel has finally replied to my email!

FROM Jeremy Schnitzel

TO Hope Jones

DATE Friday 10 January

SUBJECT Re: Plastic

ATTACHMENT Willow Group environmental audit

Dear Ms Jones

It was very good to meet you outside the shop this week.

As I said to you in person, I am very sorry that it has taken me a few days to respond to your message.

I can assure you that the company takes its environmental responsibility very seriously, and we are doing all we can to limit our use of plastics.

I am attaching a copy of our most recent environmental audit. Of course this is intended for adult readers, but I hope you will be able to understand enough of it to appreciate that we are doing our very best to help the environment.

Please don't hesitate to contact me with any further questions.

Best wishes

Jeremy Schnitzel
Branch Manager

The **Willow** Group
'Fresh food is our passion'

I tried to read the environmental audit attached to Mr Schnitzel's email, but I couldn't understand very much of it.

I asked Dad to explain it to me. He knows all about things like that. But he wouldn't.

He said he has to spend all week reading reports and isn't he allowed some time off on Saturday morning.

I said couldn't he at least read the email from Mr Schnitzel. So he did. When he had read it, he said, 'Fine words butter no parsnips.'

I asked what that meant, but he just told me to look it up. Then he went back to reading the paper.

> ### 'Fine words butter no parsnips.'
> **English proverb.**
>
> First recorded use mid-17th century: 'faire words butter noe parsnips.'
>
> **Meaning:** Parsnips are more tasty if eaten with butter. However, mere words won't make those same parsnips taste any better. Therefore the phrase means that flattery will achieve nothing and action is what matters.

Dad's right. Mr Schnitzel's environmental audit might be full of words, but he's not actually doing anything. I need to continue with my protest.

This afternoon I made a terrible mistake.

It was my friend Selma's birthday party. I would have liked to protest outside the supermarket *and* go to the party, but Mum said that wasn't possible. She said we all have to make some difficult choices in our lives, and you can't do everything, but the decision was mine.

I chose the party. I wish I hadn't.

When we got to Selma's house, I saw there were five plastic balloons hanging from the front door.

I never would have noticed them before. But now I thought to myself: what if those balloons end up in the ocean? What if they got swallowed by a dolphin or stuck in a whale? How would Selma feel about that?

Inside the house there were twenty-six more balloons. There were also plastic plates for the tea. And plastic straws. And plastic cups. And plastic forks. And a plastic tablecloth.

With twelve kids, plus three adults, that adds up to a lot of plastic. Counting it all took hours. I missed most of the movie.

'Today at this party we have wasted a hundred and forty-seven different pieces of plastic,' I told Mrs Papagiannis. 'They will go into the ocean, and poison the fish and possibly kill turtles, dolphins, walruses, and whales.'

Mrs Papagiannis sighed. Then she said, 'Would you like some more lemonade, dear?'

'Only if I can have it in a reusable cup,' I said.

Mrs Papagiannis sighed again, but she did get me a glass, and at the end of the party, she said she was proud of me for caring so much about the planet. She also said sorry for the going-home bag.

I can understand why. The bag was made of plastic. Inside was a plastic pencil sharpener in the shape of a ladybird, a plastic rubber, three balloons, two plastic pens, some sweets wrapped in plastic, and some more sweets in a little plastic bag.

That is a lot of plastic just for one party. And I was there. Using all that plastic. Instead of protesting outside the supermarket.

I had the choice. I could have done a good thing. Or a bad thing. I chose the bad thing. I feel awful.

Hope Jones' Blog

Doing the right thing is really very difficult.

I was determined to protest again today. I didn't go yesterday. I went to that stupid party instead. So I had to go today.

Luckily Dad offered to come with me. He wanted to see what all the fuss was about. Apparently he used to go on protests when he was a student, but they were really just an excuse for having a few beers with his mates.

I explained that my protest isn't anything like that, and he said he's glad to hear it.

Mum stayed at home. This morning she twisted her ankle while jogging in the park. She wanted Dad to go and buy a packet of frozen peas, but I reminded him that they come in plastic bags. So she used a wet tea towel instead.

We left Mum on the sofa, resting her ankle, while the rest of us went to the supermarket. That's me, Dad, Finn, and Becca. When we arrived, I got the biggest shock of my life. There were two people protesting already!

Please say hello to Penelope and William!

I didn't know them till today. But they knew me. Or they'd seen me here, anyway. And they had been inspired to come and protest.

Penelope said, 'We hope you don't mind.'

Obviously I didn't. We took turns to shout slogans and chat to shoppers. During the morning, more and more people came to protest with us. There were George and Bart from my school with their mum. And three other kids from Becca's school. Sparkle came with some of her friends. Quite a lot of other people stayed for five or ten minutes, or half an hour, taking turns to hold the banner.

Almost all of them took some pictures of me or did some selfies to put on Instagram and Twitter and Facebook and other social media channels.

It was brilliant.

tariq

♡ 97 likes

tariq Supermarkets need to take action to stop using so much plastic. They're killing our planet. This protest was started by a girl who lives near me. She's very inspiring!
#stopplastic #plasticfree #savetheturtles #ecowarrior #girlpower #listentothekids #greenpeace #friendsoftheearth #nextgeneration #oneplanet #gogreen #hopejones #hopejonessavestheworld

I was very surprised by Dad. He couldn't stop shouting. 'Save the planet! Stop using plastic!'

His voice is remarkably loud.

'That's because I used to be an actor,' he said.

I never knew he used to be an actor.

'There are a lot of things you don't know about me,' Dad said.

I'm beginning to realise that.

The whole day was brilliant. I was feeling so happy! Then Mrs Ahmed came past. And everything went wrong.

It wasn't her fault. She just gave me some information, which made me feel awful.

Mrs Ahmed lives on our street. She was doing her shopping with her two sons Mohammed and Joseph. They were each carrying two of those skimpy plastic bags, which fall apart as soon as you put anything heavy inside.

I said, 'You should use reusable bags instead of those ones. It's much better for the planet.'

Mrs Ahmed said I was right. She said it's difficult to find the right bags at the right moment when you're a single mother with two sons who have to be watched every minute. Then she pointed at my banner and said, 'Haven't you read about the environmental impact of glitter?'

I said I hadn't.

She said, 'Look it up.'

I did. It was awful. Glitter is literally poison for the planet. It's even worse than plastic straws or plastic bottles.

Now I'm feeling horrible. I'm guilty. I'm ashamed. I'm a bad person. I thought I was doing the right thing, but actually I've just messed up the world even more than before.

Dad said, 'Don't worry, pumpkin. You can't do everything right. We're all human. We all make mistakes. But you're doing something. You're making a difference. That's brilliant! You care about the planet. That's amazing. You should feel proud of yourself. I'm proud of you, anyway. You're the best.'

'What about me?' said Finn.

'And me!' said Becca.

'You're both the best too,' Dad said. 'Come on. Let's shout at Mr Schnitzel a bit more.'

We all shouted at the tops of our voices: 'Save the planet! Stop using plastic! Save the planet! Stop using plastic! Save the planet! Stop using plastic!'

RUBBISH DOESN'T TALK – BUT IT SAYS A LOT.

REFILL NOT LANDFILL

PLASTIC? NO, THANKS.

STOP BUYING RUBBISH – AND SHOPS WILL STOP SELLING RUBBISH

On the way home we stopped at Flat White to meet Brendan. He was just as nice as his email. His hot chocolate was delicious too. Dad said the coffee was excellent.

When things got quiet at the counter, Brendan came and sat down with us for a chat.

He grew up in Australia, but he came to live in England because he likes the rain. That's what he said, although later he admitted he was only joking, and the real reason is his girlfriend Leah, who is from here.

Brendan has three earrings in his left ear and four more in his right ear. He also has a long curly beard and a tattoo of *The Scream* by Edvard Munch on his chest. You can just see it under his shirt. I had never heard of Edvard Munch until I met Brendan, which just goes to show how educational tattoos can be. I would like to get a tattoo of a famous painting on my chest, but Mum said not over her dead body, so maybe I'll just get a dolphin on my ankle like Aunt Jess.

Brendan agreed with Dad about the glitter. Which made me feel a lot better.

He said nothing is ever perfect and you've just got to do your best. Sometimes you make mistakes. Sometimes you go backwards. Sometimes you feel like the world is against you. But you just have to keep trying.

His life has been full of difficult situations. Moving here from Australia. His mum dying. The tax bill which almost shut him down. But he kept working. He never gave up. And now Flat White is going from strength to strength.

Brendan isn't just good at making coffee. He is doing his best to encourage environmental awareness. Hot drinks are 50p off if you bring your own cup, and they are only using paper bags, not plastic. He's been researching new ways to make the café even more sustainable.

Brendan gave me a free macaron to say thank you and keep up the good work.

It was delicious.

Hope Jones' Blog

MONDAY 13 JANUARY

Hello.

It's me. Hope.

I need your help.

I can't go to the supermarket any more, because I'm grounded. So can you go instead? Can you go to your local supermarket and talk to the manager and ask them to stop using plastic? I want to do it myself. But I can't. I'm stuck at home.

It happened like this.

When I came back from school, I wanted to go straight out again, and protest at the supermarket.

But Mum said no. She didn't want to put unnecessary pressure on her ankle.

I felt so frustrated! And annoyed! The women at Greenham Common didn't have a day off. They just kept protesting every day until the Americans took their bombs away. I wanted to be the same with Mr Schnitzel. I didn't want to take a day off just because my mum needed to put her foot up.

Then I thought about my heroes. What would Mahatma Gandhi have done in my situation? Or Nelson Mandela? Or Emmeline Pankhurst?

They are my heroes because we studied them at school last term when we did 'People who changed the world and made a difference'.

They all changed the world. And made a difference. If their mums told them to stay at home and take it easy, would they have stayed at home? Of course not!

They would have said, 'Sorry, Mum, but I can't stay here right now, because I've got to do some peaceful protesting/stop apartheid/fight for women's votes.'

I didn't actually say that to Mum, because I had a pretty good idea what she would reply. Instead I just sneaked out of the house without her seeing.

I took my banner. Carrying it on my own was quite difficult. Holding it up was impossible. I thought I might have to give up and go home, but luckily I spotted a plant pot by the entrance to the supermarket. I jammed one end of my banner into it and held the other end, which worked surprisingly well.

I didn't shout as much as usual. I felt embarrassed on my own. But lots of people came to talk to me. I had met some of them before, but others were brand new. Saving the world is a great way to make friends.

Sparkle was there. She brought me a book about becoming a vegan. Apparently after reading this book, I'll never want to eat cheese again, let alone lamb chops or lasagna.

I don't know if I want to read it. Of course I want to stop pollution and climate change. But I love lasagna. And lamb chops. And cheese.

Saving the world is so complicated.

Sparkle had to go, so I was all on my own when Mum came hobbling up to me. Her face was bright red. I don't know if that was from using the crutches or being angry. Maybe both. I told her there was no need to worry, because I was perfectly safe. But she wouldn't listen. She made me roll up my banner and go straight home.

Now I'm grounded till the weekend.

I said, 'What about the planet?'

Mum said, 'The planet will have to look after itself.'

Unfortunately it can't. That's exactly the problem.

'You're only ten years old,' Mum said. 'You are not allowed to leave the house alone. Do you understand?'

I said of course I understood, but what would have happened to Mahatma Gandhi or Emmeline Pankhurst if they hadn't had the courage to break the rules sometimes.

Mum said, 'Mahatma Gandhi and Emmeline Pankhurst were not ten years old.'

'They were once,' I said.

'But not when they broke the rules.'

'You don't know that,' I said.

That was when Mum blew up. She said saving the world was all very well, but if I sneaked out of the house again, I would be grounded for the rest of the year, and this tablet would be confiscated, which would probably be a good thing anyway,

because I was spending much too much time staring at screens, and what was wrong with reading a book?

There's nothing wrong with reading a book. I love books. But I love the planet too. And I want to save it.

If you are reading this, will you do something for me? Will you please, please, go to your nearest supermarket and ask them to use less plastic?

Maybe you could make a banner. Maybe you could start a petition. Maybe you could email the branch manager. Maybe you could talk to the cashier. Or maybe you could just not buy anything which is covered in plastic. I've done all those things. I'm going to keep doing them.

I can't right now, because I'm grounded. But will you go and do them instead? Please?

Hope Jones' Blog

TUESDAY 14 JANUARY

Being grounded is extremely frustrating. I want to be outside the supermarket, changing the world. Instead I'm stuck at home, doing nothing.

I have tried to spend my time usefully, so I have been learning more about Nelson Mandela, Mahatma Gandhi, and Emmeline Pankhurst.

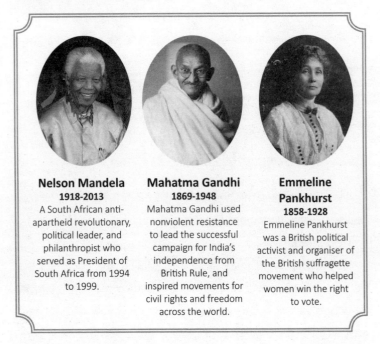

Nelson Mandela
1918-2013
A South African anti-apartheid revolutionary, political leader, and philanthropist who served as President of South Africa from 1994 to 1999.

Mahatma Gandhi
1869-1948
Mahatma Gandhi used nonviolent resistance to lead the successful campaign for India's independence from British Rule, and inspired movements for civil rights and freedom across the world.

Emmeline Pankhurst
1858-1928
Emmeline Pankhurst was a British political activist and organiser of the British suffragette movement who helped women win the right to vote.

I knew a bit. Now I know a lot more. It's been very interesting. And inspiring.

Just like me, they all got grounded.

Actually, they weren't exactly grounded. They were sent to prison. But it's more or less the same thing.

If you don't already know about Nelson Mandela and Mahatma Gandhi and Emmeline Pankhurst, you should look them up on the internet too.

At school this term our values are RESILIENCE and PERSISTENCE, and I definitely haven't seen any examples of people who have been more resilient or persistent than Nelson Mandela, Mahatma Gandhi, or Emmeline Pankhurst. They were amazing! They all thought the world was unjust, so they tried to change it.

Perhaps getting grounded (or sent to prison) is just what happens to people who try to change the world.

I don't feel so bad about being grounded any more. In fact I feel quite good about it.

I am in a long tradition of people who tried to change the world. Nelson Mandela, Mahatma Gandhi, Emmeline Pankhurst, and Hope Jones – all of us have been grounded for our beliefs and our persistence and our resilience and our determination to change the world.

The only problem is I can't continue my protest. Mr Schnitzel will think I've given up. But I really haven't. I'm just counting the days till I'm released from prison.

Hope Jones' Blog

Today at school I had a very interesting conversation with Harry. He doesn't agree with me about civil disobedience. He thinks it is always important to obey the law and that we must stay within the boundaries set for us by society, however unjust or iniquitous they might seem.

I know he uses long words, but that's just what he's like. What he means is he doesn't think we should do anything which might get us sent to prison or grounded.

But he does absolutely agree with me about plastic. And he's been doing something brilliant about it.

In fact, I think he might have been doing something even better than me. He said he has been inspired by my campaign. His mum and dad have too. They have bought reusable water bottles and refillable shampoo bottles. His father has started shaving with an electric razor and his mother has started ordering milk in glass bottles. Rather than shopping at a supermarket, they now go to a special bulk buy shop, where you can fill your own containers with rice and pasta and washing-up liquid.

In the past eight days they have saved 103 items of single-use plastic that they would otherwise have used.

I was very impressed.

I wish I had made a spreadsheet like his, but I don't know how to. Harry is going to give me a lesson as soon as he has a moment.

Harry might not share my beliefs about peaceful protests and civil disobedience, but he is extremely good at saving the planet.

The Murakami family: a record of the plastic that we have <u>NOT</u> used.	
Straws	4
Water bottles	9
Milk cartons	5
Cups	11
Knives, forks and spoons	3
Razors	2
Toothbrushes	3
Packaging	37
Takeaway boxes	1
Cotton buds	17
Cling film	1 roll
Ready meals	1
Miscellaneous	9
Total	**103**

16th January

Dear Mr Crabbe

I am very sorry for being rude to you this morning. I don't really think you're a stupid old man. I shouldn't have said that to you. It just slipped out because I was so cross. No one has ever called me a bossy young woman before, or told me to stop sticking my nose into other people's business, and I was very surprised, and to be honest quite annoyed. But I still shouldn't have called you a stupid old man. I'm very sorry I did.

I actually wasn't being bossy. Or sticking my nose into your business. I was just trying to be neighbourly. I thought you might have forgotten that Thursday is rubbish day, so I wanted to remind you to put out your recycling bins.

I know you don't care about recycling. I know you don't care about the planet either. You told me that several times. However, I do care about the planet. And I live here too. I don't want the whole planet to be covered in your plastic waste and your old tins and your old cans and your beer bottles which you can't be bothered to recycle.

Page 1 of 2

101

I'm very sorry if that sounds rude. Or bossy. Maybe it is rude and bossy. But it's still true.

Two weeks ago, you asked me what the planet had ever done for you. On that day (Thursday 2nd January), I was too surprised to reply properly. I have now had some time to think about my answer.

The planet made you, Mr Crabbe. You wouldn't even be here without it. Nor would your house. Or your car. Or your clothes. Or the air that you breathe. Or the food that you eat. Or any of the people who you know and love. They are all part of this planet. So are you. So am I. That's why we have to look after it.

Yours sincerely,

Hope Jones

(from next door)

Hope Jones' Blog

FRIDAY 17 JANUARY

Mum, if you're reading this, I'm sorry.

I'm very sorry.

I really am extremely sorry.

I know I'm grounded. I know I'm not allowed to leave the house. I know you're going to be furious with me. I know, I know, I know. But I had to go and meet Tariq and Claude.

I didn't go alone. Becca took me. She's sorry too. But it was worth it. Look:

That is me and Claude sitting on the steps outside the supermarket doing our interview.

103

I felt very bad about not telling you, Mum. But I knew you'd say no.

You would have done, wouldn't you? Go on, admit it. You know you would. That's why I had to sneak out of the house with Becca. It's not her fault. She made me promise to say that. But it's also true.

This morning Becca got a text from Tariq saying his friend Claude wanted to interview me. Claude works for a news website. An interview with him is guaranteed at least a thousand hits.

Imagine how long it would take me to talk to a thousand people! Whereas with an interview, I can talk to them all at once.

Becca said we should probably leave it to the weekend and do it then when I wasn't grounded any more. She knew you'd say no. She didn't want to upset or annoy you. But I said we had to do it straightaway.

Sorry, Mum. But I had to. I do understand the consequences of my actions. I know I'll be grounded for longer. But Emmeline Pankhurst was arrested and sent to prison for six weeks, and she had to share her cell with rats, so I'm not complaining.

Sometimes you have to suffer for your beliefs.

Claude was really nice.

I've never done an interview before, but it wasn't difficult. I just had to answer some questions about myself and the turtles and plastic and why I think the world is such a mess. I talked about glitter, too. I think I got a bit carried away. I ended up talking about my dilemmas with the banner, and not knowing if I was doing the right thing or the wrong thing, and how difficult it is, just being one small person in such a big world, wanting to make things better, but not exactly knowing how.

Right at the end, I remembered my blog. I said please come and visit **hopejonessavestheworld.com** and find out more about me and why I'm trying to save the world.

After the interview was over, when Claude had switched off the camera, he said I was a natural communicator.

I hope he's right. Because if a thousand people watch my interview, and all of them stop using glitter and plastic bags and plastic wrapping and plastic straws, then together we really could make a difference.

He's going to edit the interview this weekend and put it up on his site. I'll link to it here so you can watch it too.

Hope Jones' Blog

MONDAY 20 JANUARY

Hello!

It's me again. Hope. I'm back. Did you think I'd given up? Or gone away? I hadn't. I just had my computer privileges removed. And I've been grounded until the end of the month.

I know. I know. Life isn't fair. But what can you do when you're only ten?

I'll tell you one thing you can do. You can use the computers at school. Especially if your best friend is Harry Murakami and he knows the supply teacher's password.

Thanks, Harry!

You probably want to know about why I was grounded this time, so I'll tell you the whole story.

When Mum found out that Becca and I had sneaked out of the house together, she was absolutely furious. In fact she was more furious than I've ever seen her before, and I have seen her being really quite furious. This time she was so angry that she literally couldn't speak. Her cheeks turned pink. She burst into tears. Then she didn't say anything for a long time. That was the worst thing. It would have been much easier if she'd just shouted at us. But she didn't. She just sat there with her hands over her face. Finally she lifted her head and looked at us and said she was a terrible mother. We told her she wasn't, but she didn't seem to care. She just spoke to us very quietly and said some things which made me burst into tears too.

It was horrible.

I know Mum might be reading this. And if she is, she'll probably ground me for another month and stop my computer privileges for the rest of the year. I still have to do it.

Sorry, Mum.

But there's something I have to say.

Claude has edited the interview. It looks amazing. I want you to see it. I want everyone to see it.

I've emailed it to all nineteen contacts in my address book and asked them to forward it to everyone they know. Will you do that too?

1.20 / 3.40   38 views

I don't know when I'll be able to use a computer again. I need your help. Even if I can't go and protest myself, at least people can watch my interview, and be inspired to do it too.

Apparently it's already doing really well. Claude sent me a message to say eleven people watched it on the first day and twenty-seven more watched it yesterday. That's thirty-eight altogether.

I don't know how many people watched it today. I'm still waiting to hear from him. But Harry has calculated that if the numbers continue accelerating at the same rate as day one and day two, a hundred people will have seen it by the end of the week.

A hundred people!

If I spent a day outside the supermarket, I probably wouldn't speak to as many people as that. Technology is amazing.

Bye for now.

Love from

Hope

WEDNESDAY 22 JANUARY

Hello! It's me again. Hope. I've got some big news. I've gone viral.

Dad said, 'Does that mean you've caught something?'

His jokes get worse and worse.

'You have to try,' Dad said.

We told him he doesn't.

When I checked my messages, I had one from Claude. He said my interview had been watched by:

11 people on the first day.

27 on the second.

503 on the third day.

More than two thousand on the fourth day.

Which altogether makes about three thousand people.

Which you might think is a lot.

It is a lot. I've probably never met as many as three thousand people in my entire life.

But wait.

Just wait.

How many people do you think have watched it today?

Guess.

Go on. Have a guess.

Did you guess?

Ok.

Was this your guess:

Can you believe it???

It's not even the end of the day, but already thirty-seven thousand, nine hundred and twelve people have watched my interview with Claude!

Even if I stood outside the supermarket with my banner for a whole year, I wouldn't be able to talk to that many people. But they've all watched my interview today. They know what I think about the world. They know what I think about Mr Schnitzel. They know what I think about plastic. They know who I am.

Wow. Thirty-seven thousand, nine hundred, and twelve. That really is a lot of people.

And it's only teatime. Imagine how many people might have watched it by the end of the day! Imagine how many people might watch it tomorrow!

Being viral is literally the most exciting thing that has ever happened to me. It is the most exciting thing that's ever happened to Becca and Finn too, and they aren't even the ones going viral. Both of them have been telling all their friends to watch the video. And telling their friends to tell their friends.

Claude says it is unlike anything he's ever seen before. He says the website can hardly cope, and if these visitor numbers go much higher he'll have to move to a new server.

I felt bad about that, but apparently it's a good thing.

Have you watched our interview? If not, please watch it right now. You'll enjoy it. I promise. And when you've watched it, please send it to all your friends and relations. I want to go even more viral.

As you can see, I'm back on my tablet again. I don't even have to use the school computer.

Mum and I had a long conversation about personal responsibility. She said I need to understand the consequences of my actions. I said I already do. I understand that if I throw away a plastic bag, it will live in the ocean for hundreds of years. I'll be dead. My children will be dead. My children's children's children's children's children's children's children will be dead. But that plastic bag will still be floating around the ocean. And it will very probably kill a turtle or a seagull. I understand that if I had used a reusable bag instead, my actions would not have the consequence of killing a turtle or a seagull.

If only other people understood the consequences of their actions a bit better, the world wouldn't be in such a mess. By other people, I mean especially grown-ups.

Grown-ups are the ones who don't seem to understand the consequences of their actions at all. They keep messing up the world. They build big houses and drive big cars and fly planes and dump rubbish everywhere without thinking about anything.

Mum sighed. Then she told me that I have to take responsibility for my own actions in every way, not just environmentally, and I have to understand the consequences of sneaking out of the house, especially when I'm already grounded.

It sounds as if we were disagreeing, but actually we weren't.

We agreed about a lot of things. Basically we're on the same side. That's what we realised.

Mum cares about the planet. She just cares about the safety of her children even more. So we reached an agreement.

I promised never to leave the house again without telling her where I was going, whatever Nelson Mandela, Mahatma Gandhi, and Emmeline Pankhurst might have done.

Mum said they were grown-ups when they were changing the world, and I can do whatever I want when I'm a grown-up, but right now I'm only a kid, so I have to follow her rules.

Being ten really is very frustrating. Becca says being a teenager is even worse. Maybe it's only the grown-ups who are happy. Maybe they're so busy being happy that they can't clear up after themselves. That would explain why they've made such a mess of the world.

Hope Jones' Blog

THURSDAY 23 JANUARY

Today was recycling day.

I don't know if Mr Crabbe read my letter last week. He never replied. He didn't put out any recycling today.

I don't know what to do. Should I send him another letter? Or should I just leave him alone?

Going viral is quite strange. Today, for instance, Jemima told me that she had watched my interview on the internet. She said a friend of a friend of her mum's had forwarded it to her. Apparently they didn't even know me and Jemima were at the same school. They were just interested in what I was saying. They had been sent it by someone else who doesn't know me or Jemima either.

All around the world, people are watching my interview.

Jemima said I should think about having a haircut before doing any more interviews. She can recommend an excellent personal stylist who will come to your house.

I said thanks, but no thanks.

Appearances aren't important. What matters is what you think and what you say and what you do. Not what you look like.

When I came home from school and checked my messages, I had twenty-seven.

That's more than I usually get in a week.

Actually, it's more than I usually get in a year.

Mum said, 'I'd better read them first. In case they're from crazy people.'

Becca said, 'Of course they're from crazy people. Who else would want to write to her?'

Some of them were from crazy people. But the others made perfect sense. One of them was from Aunt Jess. She sent a link and said, 'Is this you?????'

I wrote back, 'Yes!!!!!'

The internet is amazing. I haven't been back to the supermarket since last Wednesday, but even so people all around the world know about my protest.

I also had a message from a man in the Netherlands who

says I have won twelve million dollars and could I please contact him to claim my share of the prize.

Becca says she gets those emails all the time and you should just delete it. So I did.

Finn said, 'But what if she really has?'

'She hasn't,' Becca said.

'But what if she has?'

I'm sure Becca is right. Even so I can't stop thinking about those twelve million dollars. Imagine how many turtles I could save with that.

☐☆▷	Jessica Buswell	**Proud Auntie!** Is this you?????
☐☆▷	Sarah Kent	**Go Eco Girl** Oh wow, just seen your interview. So inspiring . . .
☐☆▷	Tom Edney	**Local councillor** Dear Miss Jones, I was delighted to see your video online. At the council we . . .
☐☆▷	Aarav Mukherjee	**It's our future** Hi Hope, I'm ten years old too and I've been trying to stop using so much plastic . . .
☐☆▷	Sem DeJong	**You're a winner !!!** Hi Hope, You have won $12,000,000. Claim your prize . . .
☐☆▷	Harry Murakami	**Have you seen the views now?!** I can't believe how many views you have – wow! You're really getting . . .
☐☆▷	Aisha McMillan	**Hi Hope!** Aah! Can't believe you've gone viral!! So cool! Love your blog.

Hope Jones' Blog

I'm sorry if you sent me a message and I haven't replied to it. I've been very busy. And I've had a lot of messages.

When I got home from school and checked my emails, I had a hundred and twelve.

Mum said she has to read them first to weed out the crazy ones, but she hasn't got time at the moment, because she's got to make the fish pie, and hang up the washing, not to mention finish the homework for her course.

I said when will she have time, and she said maybe at the weekend. By then I'll probably have thousands.

Luckily Dad was more interested. When he came home from work, he said of course he would read my messages, and we should use this momentum to force some serious change. He had that wild sparkling look in his eyes that he sometimes gets on holidays when he's just about to make us all climb a mountain or eat a dish on the menu which no one can translate.

The look had faded a bit after he'd read fifty of my messages. It had gone completely by the time he'd read a hundred. But he didn't give up. He's not the giving-up type. His middle name is Perseverance. (It's actually Stephen.)

Dad read all a hundred and thirty-six messages before tea. (Twenty-four more had arrived since he started.) He said roughly ten percent were from nutters and another ten percent were frankly abusive, so he deleted them immediately. But the remaining eighty percent were broadly supportive and showed I had touched a nerve.

If you sent me a message – thank you!

If you're reading this – thank you!

If you watched my interview with Claude – thank you!

If you sent it to all your friends and relations – thank you!

Together we can change the world.

Hope Jones' Blog

Today has been a very interesting day.

I was high-fived by a stranger. And I had an idea for the next stage of my protest.

I don't want to be like the women at Greenham Common and carry on protesting for nineteen years. I don't have time for that. Nineteen years from now, our planet will have been overwhelmed by plastic. Think of all the turtles that will have died. All the seals and walruses too. We have to make some changes right now. Today. Or at least this week.

That's what I want to say to Mr Schnitzel. Unfortunately I didn't see him today. He might have been hiding at the back of his shop. Or perhaps he's having the weekend off.

Anyway, you're probably wondering how I was high-fived by a stranger and had a new idea for my protest. So I'll tell you.

Dad took me and Becca to the supermarket with my banner.

We had only just started protesting when a man came over and gave me a high-five.

'Go, girl!' he said.

It was quite surprising, because I had never seen him before. But he knew all about me. He had watched my interview three times. He had also sent it to his nieces in Cornwall, who go out once a month to clear up the rubbish on their local beach. He said they have been inspired by my protest and they are going to write to the branch manager of their local supermarket too.

Hello,
Skye and Isla
in St Agnes!

Then two women called Ruth and Amanda asked if they could take selfies with me.

They said they loved my interview and I was an inspiration to young people everywhere. They are both from South Africa, but they're working as nurses here for a year. They told me about the water crisis in Cape Town, which sounds terrible.

All afternoon more people came to talk to me. Several of them joined the protest too. Lots more took selfies.

Tariq was there too. He talked to Becca for ages. She couldn't stop smiling after he left. She didn't want to tell me why, but eventually she admitted he had invited her to go to the movies tonight.

I asked if I could go too, but Becca said, 'You must be joking.'

Dad said I could go to the cinema with Harry.

Obviously it won't be a date, but I don't care. I would just like to go to a movie.

The morning went past in a flash. Suddenly it was almost lunchtime. We had to go home to meet Mum and Finn. Dad wanted to leave me and Becca outside while he nipped into the supermarket to buy a few things.

I said he must be joking.

Didn't he remember what we were doing?

Even Mum has been boycotting the supermarket!

Dad said, 'That's Mum, not me. Sorry, Hope. I know it's a bit hypocritical. But I haven't got all day. I just want to nip in there and buy some bread and a chicken. I've got my own bag.'

I reminded him that we could go to buy bread from the bakery and a chicken from Mitch the butcher.

'We need some potatoes,' Dad said. 'And veg too. Maybe some broccoli. And some carrots.'

'We could get them from Bosphorus,' I said.

Bosphorus is the Turkish shop, which has amazing dates and olives, and just about every vegetable you can imagine.

Dad said, 'This is going to take all day.'

In the end, it only took about forty-five minutes. And it was a lot more fun than going to the supermarket.

I had a good conversation with Mitch the butcher. He said he has to use some plastic bags to keep the meat fresh and germ-free, but he's determined to cut down as much as possible.

Bosphorus is run by a man called Mr Zaimoglu. I had never actually talked to him before, although I had seen him unloading all the boxes of mangoes and plums and aubergines and olives.

I had a lot of questions. For instance: why does the supermarket wrap all its fruit and veg in plastic, but not him?

Mr Zaimoglu gave me a long explanation, which I didn't exactly understand. But basically he said the supermarket saves money by using more plastic. Which seems the wrong way round to me.

From now on we're going to shop at Bosphorus and the butcher and the baker instead of the supermarket.

Back at home, Becca spent three hours getting ready for her date with Tariq. I don't ever want to be a teenager. It's all such a waste of time.

While she was doing that, and Dad was cooking tea, I made a new banner.

I recycled the sticks from the old banner and the old sheet went back in the cupboard with the DIY stuff for next time Dad paints a room.

Dad had bought me some biodegradable glitter on the internet. It's made from leaves and looks just as good as ordinary glitter.

Hope Jones' Blog

SUNDAY 26 JANUARY

Today Becca took me to the supermarket with my new banner. She was in a good mood because of her date with Tariq. Apparently it went very well indeed. I asked if that meant they kissed and she said it was a state secret.

She's always telling Dad off for joking, but really she's no better herself.

The supermarket opens at ten o'clock on a Sunday morning. We arrived at quarter past, and there were already eleven people there.

I don't mean eleven people shopping at the supermarket. I mean eleven people waiting at my protest. It's not even my protest any more. It's our protest.

They were all really nice. I knew William and Penelope already, and Gareth and his dog Muffin, but the others were new. They all really liked my banner. Especially when they heard the glitter is biodegradable.

It was more like a party than a protest. Penelope had made cupcakes. We sang songs together. We stopped people who were going into the supermarket and talked to them about plastic and recycling and saving the planet.

It was brilliant!

Only one person didn't enjoy it. That was Mr Schnitzel. He asked us to go away and protest somewhere else, but we said no.

'You're affecting my business,' Mr Schnitzel said. 'Footfall is down by seven percent. If you don't move away from these premises, I'm going to call the police. You're leaving me no other option.'

Becca was beginning to look a bit nervous, but I wasn't worried. I already knew what the police would do.

'This is a public pavement,' I said. 'I'm allowed here just as much as you are.'

At that moment, Mrs Ahmed came over with Mo and Joe. She asked what my banner meant. I explained that if she did her shopping at Mitch the butcher and Bosphorus and the bakery, she would be saving the planet, and then she could pop into Flat White and Brendan might even give her a free macaron.

'That all sounds brilliant,' Mrs Ahmed said. 'There's just one problem. This place is so much cheaper.'

'Convenience is our middle name,' Mr Schnitzel said. 'Don't forget we've got some great offers at the moment. Three for two on all frozen ready meals. You could stock up your freezer.'

I said, 'Ready meals aren't good for you. They're full of salt and preservatives. And they're terrible for the environment. You should buy fresh fruit and vegetables at Bosphorus instead.'

'I've got two kids and a job,' said Mrs Ahmed. 'Ready meals save my life.'

'What about the planet?' I said. 'Don't you care about the planet?'

'Of course I do,' said Mrs Ahmed. 'I'm just busy all the time. I'm swept off my feet. If you could persuade my sons to lend a hand around the house, I'd have time to cook them a proper tea instead of those ready meals.'

I had a quiet word with Joe and Mo. They both agreed. So it was settled. I know they only really cared about the free macarons, but so what? Doing the right thing is still doing the right thing even if you're only doing it for a free macaron.

When they'd gone, Mr Schnitzel wagged his finger at me. 'You'll be hearing from our lawyers,' he said.

I don't care. The law is on my side. I'm allowed to protest outside his supermarket. The police have already said so. I bet a lawyer will too.

When they had gone, Becca had a brilliant idea. She said we shouldn't lecture people or tell them off. It only makes them cross. Instead we asked them to buy one less bit of plastic. Just one. That's all.

Take one piece of plastic out of your shopping basket and put it back on the shelf and replace it with something that doesn't use plastic.

You know what? My sister is a genius. It really worked.

No one likes being lectured. Or told off. But people don't mind if you ask them to buy one less piece of plastic.

And if everyone bought one less . . .

. . . Think how much plastic we would save!

Hope Jones' Blog

SUNDAY 26 JANUARY

I've just been through my emails with Dad. I had two hundred and eighty-seven.

Dad said it was enough to make him give up his New Year's resolution. Luckily there isn't any beer in the house or I think he probably would have.

Anyway, I haven't heard from the supermarket's lawyers. But I have heard from Ginny Tuffington-Pertwhistle, who works for the Willow Group of supermarkets. Mr Schnitzel must have given her my address.

FROM Ginny Tuffington-Pertwhistle
TO Hope Jones
DATE Sunday 26 January
SUBJECT We love turtles!!!!!

Hi Hope

I work at the Head Office of the Willow Group of
Supermarkets, and I have to tell you, we're very impressed
by what you've been doing.

We've all seen your amazing protest, and – wow!!!
It's wonderful that you feel so passionately about the
environment.

Here at Willow Supermarkets, we feel passionately about
the environment too, and we'd love to find a way to work
together. Do you have a number I could call you on?

Ginny
Ginny Tuffington-Pertwhistle
Head of Publicity and Public Relations

The **Willow** Group
'Fresh food is our passion'

I emailed her back with Mum's number and she rang it
immediately. She has invited us to Head Office. She says she can't
wait to meet me. I can't wait to meet her either. I hope she's got
good news. I hope she's going to say that the Willow Group is
going to ban plastic from all its supermarkets.

Hope Jones' Blog

MONDAY 27 JANUARY

A million people have watched the interview.

That's right. A million.

2.50 / 3.40   1,000,007 views

Becca said it must be exhausting being famous.

I told her not to be silly. But I'm beginning to think she might be right. Maybe I am becoming a little bit famous.

On the way to school, Mrs Goldstein stopped to tell me that her nephew in Leeds has seen my interview. He has been inspired and he's going to stop using plastic too.

Someone waved at me from a van. I didn't recognise her. But she knew my name. She shouted, 'Are you Hope? The one who's saving the world?'

I said yes.

She said, 'Go girl! We're with you!'

Everyone at school knows about my campaign. Even my teacher, Miss Brockenhurst.

She said perhaps I could do an assembly about political activism.

I said I didn't know the first thing about political activism.

She said that's clearly not true.

I said I don't even know what political activism means.

She just laughed.

But I don't.

Jemima Higginbotham said her uncle is a member of parliament and if Miss Brockenhurst wanted to hear from someone who really knew about politics, why didn't we ask him to come and speak to us?

Miss Brockenhurst said, 'That's a great idea, Jemima. When you next speak to your uncle, will you ask him to come and speak to the school? But I'd like Hope to speak to us, too. We're all citizens, aren't we? We all live in this country. We all share the resources of this planet. You, me, your mums, your dads, your neighbours, the prime minister – we all live here together. I hope we'll all get the chance to tell our stories. So, Hope, could you do that? Could you say a few words at assembly on Friday morning?'

I said no problem.

Miss Brockenhurst says the school council elections are later this term and will I apply?

I'm definitely going to.

I'll have to give a speech to the whole class, which will be embarrassing, but Harry promised to help me write it.

There's just one problem. Jemima Higginbotham wants to apply, too, and she's very popular. But I hope everyone will vote for me instead.

Actually, Harry should really be on the school council instead of me or Jemima Higginbotham. He might not be going viral, but his spreadsheet is now quite enormous. He and his mum and dad have saved three hundred and ninety-one plastic items by not using them.

He's much better at saving the world than me.

Harry says that's not true, and we all have different skills, and everyone has to do what they can, and if we work together, we can make the world a better place.

I hope he's right.

The Murakami family:
a record of the plastic that we have <u>NOT</u> used.

Straws	9
Water bottles	21
Milk cartons	15
Cups	18
Knives, forks and spoons	9
Razors	4
Toothbrushes	3
Toothpaste	2
Glitter	1
Mum's stuff	29
Pens	6
Cereal	3
Shopping bags	2
Food packaging	78
Other packing	21
Crisp packets	7
Sweet packets	11
Takeaway boxes	3
Cotton buds	29
Cling film	2 rolls
Ready meals	4
Miscellaneous	83
Party poppers	1
Balloons	3
Air fresheners	2
Cleaning products	11
Dry cleaning	8
Car stuff	4
Computer stuff	2
	Total 391

Tomorrow I've got a day off school, because Mum and I are going to the Head Office of the Willow Group to meet Ginny Tuffington-Pertwhistle.

Mum got special permission from Mr Khan for me to miss school. He usually only gives special permission for funerals and dentists, but Mum persuaded him that meeting Ginny Tuffington-Pertwhistle would be educational, and luckily he agreed.

Hope Jones' Blog

TUESDAY 28 JANUARY

Hello, we're on our way to meet Ginny at the headquarters of the Willow Group.

What is she going to say to us?

I don't know. But I hope she'll say all their supermarkets are going to stop using plastic. That would be so great!

Wish me luck. I'll be back later and I'll tell you exactly what happened.

TUESDAY 28 JANUARY

Today I visited the Head Office of the Willow Group. It was a very extraordinary experience. But not in a good way. In fact it has been quite horrible. It all started well. I was really excited. The train journey was brilliant. Mum and I couldn't stop talking. We had so many ideas about what might happen.

This is us outside Head Office.

Ginny was waiting for us by the revolving doors. She gave me a big hug and a badge with my name on.

Mum got a badge too, but no hug.

Ginny is very nice. She never stops smiling. She said we'd better hurry, because they were waiting for us upstairs in the conference room.

'They?' I said. 'Who's they?'

'Mr Willow,' Ginny said, as if it was obvious.

In the lift, Ginny told us about Mr Willow. He is the grandson of the man who started the Willow Group of supermarkets. Because he was someone's grandson, I thought he would be about the same age as me, but in fact he was an old man with white hair.

Herbert Willow

chief executive

The **Willow** Group
'Fresh food is our passion'

The conference room was on the twenty-third floor. The view was amazing. You can see the whole city. I would have liked to stand there and look out of the window for ages, but there wasn't time. Mr Willow is a very busy man. He shook my hand and said, 'It's such a pleasure to meet you.'

I said it was very nice to meet him too.

Mr Schnitzel wasn't there. He had to stay in the store and deal with customers. Instead there were two women from the Marketing Department and a man from Sales and a woman called Janine who is the Vice-President of Sustainability at the Willow Group.

There was also a photographer, who wanted to take a photo of me with Mr Willow, but Mum wouldn't let him. She didn't want my image used for any publicity or marketing purposes.

We all sat down at the long table. Mr Willow said he had enjoyed my interview.

I tried to explain it wasn't exactly meant to be enjoyable, but he wasn't really listening to me.

He said they had been listening carefully to the thoughts and needs of customers like myself, and they were planning to change their environmental policy before the end of the year.

I said it's only January, so the end of the year is actually a very long way away.

Mr Willow said he could assure me that significant changes would be made in the very near future.

I said, 'Like what exactly?'

He said they were currently drawing up a comprehensive report with a range of recommendations, which could be implemented in the short to medium term.

I said, 'Fine words butter no parsnips.'

Mr Willow said he knew exactly what I meant and so the Willow Group was intending to give ten thousand pounds to a charity which did great work saving turtles.

'That's very nice of you,' I said. 'But the turtles don't need your money. What they need is less plastic in the ocean.'

'Ten thousand pounds will make a lot of difference,' said Mr Willow.

I said, 'Do you think it will save the turtles?'

Mr Willow said he hoped so.

I said I did too. But I thought it probably wouldn't. And it would be better for the turtles, the seals, the seabirds, and the planet in general if he could stop using so much plastic in his supermarkets. He was the boss. Why couldn't he tell his shops to stop using plastic?

Mr Willow said he absolutely agreed, and there was nothing he cared about more than the future of our planet, and the Willow Group would soon begin a concerted effort to remove all plastic wrapping from the fresh food in their stores nationwide.

I didn't really believe him. It was like he was talking a lot, but he wasn't actually saying anything. I wanted to ask him a lot more questions. About what they would actually do. And when. If they cared so much about the turtles, why couldn't they spend a bit more money on saving them? Ten thousand pounds might be a lot for an ordinary person, but it can't be much if you own all those supermarkets.

I asked all these questions. I even said the thing about ten thousand pounds not being very much if you own so many supermarkets. Mr Willow didn't answer me. Instead he muttered something to Ginny under his breath so I couldn't hear it.

She nodded and said, 'Yes, of course, right away.'

Ginny rushed off to the corner of the room and came back with an enormous piece of cardboard printed to look like a cheque with TEN THOUSAND POUNDS written in big letters. She asked if Mr Willow and I could have our photo taken beside it.

Mum reminded her that she didn't want my image to be used for publicity or marketing purposes.

Mr Willow said, 'What's the point of her being here if we can't have a photo together?'

I said, 'The point of me being here is to talk about you using too much plastic in your shops.'

Mr Willow said, 'I've had quite enough lectures from you, young lady.'

I said I wasn't lecturing him. I was just asking him to think about the future of the planet.

Mr Willow shook his head. 'You sound just like my granddaughter. She's always going on about chuffing global warming.'

I said his granddaughter sounded very sensible and maybe he should try listening to her.

Mr Willow said he'd had just about enough of being bossed around by young women, and maybe Ginny should come up with some better ideas next time, or she could start looking for another job.

I said, 'Don't you even care about the planet?'

Mr Willow said, 'I'm a businessman, young lady. I care about the bottom line. Profit and loss – that's what matters to me. I'll leave worrying about the planet to you and Louise.'

I said, 'Who's Louise?'

'My granddaughter,' Mr Willow said. As if I was meant to know that already.

I said Louise sounded very nice, and I'd like to meet her one day, but I never wanted to shop in his stupid supermarket again.

Mr Willow said he was sorry to hear that, but I was free to take my custom wherever I wanted, and that was the wonderful thing about capitalism.

He shook Mum's hand, and mine too, and said it had been a pleasure to meet us both, which obviously wasn't true. Then he walked out with all the men and women in suits, and Ginny took us downstairs in the lift, and said we should keep in touch, although I don't think she really meant it. This time, she didn't give me a hug. She just rushed back to the lift, already talking on her phone.

On the train home, Mum put her arm around me, and said she hoped I didn't feel too disappointed.

I didn't want to make her feel bad, so I said I was fine.

But I actually do feel extremely disappointed. Today has been one of the most disappointing days of my entire life.

Hope Jones' Blog

WEDNESDAY 29 JANUARY

Today is a bad day. I'm feeling depressed.

I think it's because of meeting Mr Willow. He was just so horrible. Also he's made me realise I'm never going to change the world. The world is run by nasty sexist old men like him and they're never going to want to change anything.

After school, Mum and Becca offered to take me to the supermarket with my banner, but I didn't feel like it.

There's no point. I laughed at Finn for making his New Year's resolution 'playing for Manchester United', but mine was just as silly. Let's be honest, he's never going to play for Manchester United, and I'm never going to save the world.

Mum thinks I should cheer up, because no one keeps their New Year's resolutions.

I don't know if that's true.

I asked Becca if she had done her twelve resolutions, and she said only one of them, but that was the only one that mattered. She looked all dreamy when she said it so I think it has something to do with Tariq. She's meeting him again at the weekend.

Mum didn't keep hers. She gave up jogging after twisting her ankle. She's booked herself into a yoga class on Tuesday evenings instead.

Dad managed to give up alcohol until the night before last, when he had a relapse to celebrate the roundabouts project finally being put to bed.

Obviously Finn didn't do his.

So maybe I shouldn't feel so bad about not doing mine. But I do. I feel terrible.

If you have written to me recently, I'm very sorry that I haven't replied.

When I last looked at my inbox, I had seven hundred and twenty-nine unread messages.

Dad says he or Mum need to give them a quick once-over before me, but when are they ever going to have a chance to read seven hundred and twenty-nine messages?

To be honest, I don't really feel like reading any emails. Let alone seven hundred and twenty-nine.

Hope Jones' Blog

THURSDAY 30 JANUARY

Look.

Mr Crabbe's recycling containers.

Empty as always.

Hope Jones' Blog

FRIDAY 31 JANUARY

I had completely forgotten about assembly this morning.

When I got to class and hung up my coat, Miss Brockenhurst said, 'We're all looking forward to your assembly, Hope. We've just been talking about it in the staff meeting.'

My assembly?

My assembly???

MY ASSEMBLY???!!!

I had literally nine minutes to prepare.

I thought about locking myself in the loo and pretending to have a tummy bug.

Then I considered telling the truth and asking if I could do it next week instead. But I knew what Miss Brockenhurst would say. She'd suggest I just stood up and said a few words to everyone without worrying too much if they were perfect or not.

I imagined getting up in front of the whole school and having nothing to say. Nothing at all. Just standing there with my mouth open and no words coming out. Someone would giggle. Then people would start chortling. Until the whole school was rolling around on the floor, laughing at me.

I was beginning to panic. I think I actually would have done, but at the last moment, Harry came to the rescue.

He lent me his spreadsheet.

Luckily he had already printed it out. He had even done a pie chart with different colours to show the proportions of different types of plastic that his family had saved.

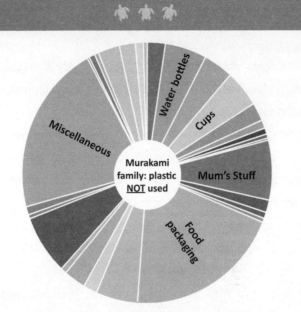

Harry suggested I should show it to everyone and talk about my resolution. So that was exactly what I did.

I always thought I was allergic to public speaking, but it turns out that I'm a natural. That's what Mr Khan said anyway.

I started by doing exactly what Harry had suggested. I held up the pie chart so the whole school could see and explained how much plastic Harry and his family had saved by not using it.

Their current total is 511 different plastic items, which is really quite amazing.

I explained about my New Year's resolution.

I told the whole school about Harry's mum's aunt and Greenham Common and making my banner.

I explained about the supermarket and Mr Schnitzel and Claude's interview and shopping local and the macarons and my trip to the headquarters of the Willow Group.

I told them about the cheque for ten thousand pounds and Mr Willow saying he didn't care about chuffing global warming.

I explained how depressed I had been feeling after my meeting with Mr Willow, because I thought I'd never be able to save the world. I thought the whole thing was hopeless. I thought I might as well give up now and just sit back and do nothing. But then Harry made me realise I was wrong. He and his family have done something amazing. They've saved 511 different plastic items.

If they could, I could too. And so could everyone else.

I said, 'We don't all have to do as much as Harry and his family. Not everyone can save 511 different plastic items. But everyone could save one. Or two. Or five. Or ten. Imagine if we all saved ten different plastic items. Imagine if everyone in this room – every single person – saved ten plastic items that they would otherwise have used. It could be a plastic cup. Or a plastic straw. Or a plastic bag. Let's all save ten each. If we all did that, together we'd save literally thousands. And then, together, we really could save the world!'

To my surprise, the whole school started cheering and clapping. Including all the teachers.

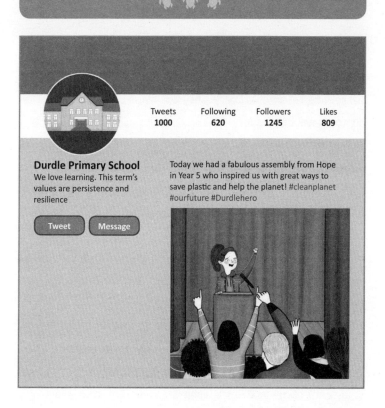

Tweets **1000**   Following **620**   Followers **1245**   Likes **809**

Durdle Primary School
We love learning. This term's values are persistence and resilience

Tweet   Message

Today we had a fabulous assembly from Hope in Year 5 who inspired us with great ways to save plastic and help the planet! #cleanplanet #ourfuture #Durdlehero

Mr Khan said, 'I want to thank you, Hope, for a wonderful assembly. You are an inspiration to us all.'

I felt so embarrassed, I wanted to sink into the floor and disappear.

But at the same time, secretly I felt quite pleased.

Maybe I really am a natural at public speaking. I don't know. But I can tell you one thing for sure: I have inspired the whole school to care more about the environment.

That's what Mr Khan said. He said we're going green.

This term we are going to devote ourselves to recycling and conserving resources. Every class will focus on a different issue and ours will be plastic.

Mr Khan asked me to do another assembly before half-term. He wants me to give concrete examples of small steps that make big changes. For example having a reusable water bottle instead of buying a plastic one. Or carrying your own cutlery instead of using plastic spoons and forks.

I said he should really ask Harry not me, because Harry is so much better than me at saving plastic, but Mr Khan said why didn't we do it together. So we're going to.

In class, Miss Brockenhurst said my assembly was extremely inspiring, and she wants everyone to follow my example.

We all drew our own spreadsheets on paper, so we can take them home and start filling them in. Obviously electronic spreadsheets are more efficient, but not everyone has their own computers at home.

You could make your own spreadsheet, too. It's very easy. You just draw some lines on a piece of paper and write down all the plastic that you've saved.

Mr Khan came to see what we were doing. He was so inspired, he put a spreadsheet in this week's newsletter, so everyone can save more plastic at home.

Durdle Primary
newsletter

Week ending: Friday 31 January

It's been another fabulous week at Durdle. Year 2 went to the train station and learnt all about gritting. Unfortunately Year 4's trip to the mosque had to be cancelled, but we're hoping to rearrange as soon as possible. Special congratulations to Gemma in Swallows for her beautiful picture of the Great Barrier Reef. A big Durdle thank you to Hope in Otters who gave an inspiring assembly on the subject of plastic. She gave us lots of brilliant ideas for us all to be eco-heroes, including this spreadsheet. Please cut it out and use it at home this week. As Hope reminded us so eloquently, we only have one planet, and we have to take good care of it. Have a lovely weekend – and try not to use any plastic! Mr Khan.

Hope and Harry from Otters, our two eco-warriors!

FAMILY NAME:

A record of the plastic that we have <u>NOT</u> used.

PLASTIC ITEM	AMOUNT NOT USED
	Total

Hope Jones' Blog

SATURDAY 1 FEBRUARY

Today's protest was the biggest yet! It was the best protest party ever. Obviously it was plastic-free. Everyone brought their own cups and plates and cutlery. Gareth brought some plastic-free balloons. They are made from latex, which is completely natural and biodegradable. They didn't actually work very well, but we had fun blowing them up.

Penelope had made brownies. Vegan, obviously, so Sparkle could have one.

We all sang songs. Some people even danced.

Harry's mum said it was much more fun than Greenham Common. She's going to send a picture to her aunt.

Only one person didn't enjoy the party. You can guess who that was. Yes. That's right. Mr Schnitzel. He came out of the supermarket and marched straight up to me.

'I thought you'd agreed to stop this,' he said.

I don't know where he heard that. Because I never agreed anything with anyone. Especially not with Mr Willow.

Mr Schnitzel asked us to move further away from the entrance to his store.

I said no.

Mr Schnitzel got even crosser. He waved his arms and shouted at me.

I just smiled back.

Eventually he went away. There was nothing else he could do.

We're not breaking the law. We're just protesting on the pavement. And having a bit of a party. Anyone is allowed to do that. It's a free country.

Claude wanted to know why I've been ignoring him. Apparently he's emailed me about seventeen times.

I haven't been ignoring him. I just haven't had a chance to read my emails. I've been completely overwhelmed.

He wants to do another interview. Apparently I've inspired copycat protests not just around the country, but in other countries around the world. Now we have to build on the momentum.

I told him I don't want to do an interview. I want to make a film. A whole proper film. Not just about me. But about other people, too. About why everyone should buy stuff from their local shop rather than using a supermarket.

I want to do an interview with Mr Zaimoglu in Bosphorus, and Mitch the butcher, and Katya in the bakery. Claude thinks it's a brilliant idea. He's going to come back next week and we'll make the film together.

After we'd finished the protest, Brendan invited us for free smoothies in Flat White. His girlfriend Leah was there too.

She's had to come and work in the café, because they've been overwhelmed with customers since I sent people his way.

I explained I hadn't exactly sent people his way. I had just suggested to people that they go to local shops and cafés rather than buying stuff from big supermarkets.

Brendan said, 'Exactly, mate! You sent them here. And I'm dead grateful. Which is why I want to give you some free smoothies.'

I had a Sunshine PickMeUp (watermelon and mango and strawberry with a dash of lime).

It was delicious. Next time you're passing Flat White, you should go and try one.

Brendan said, 'You deserve it, mate. You're an inspiration. You've changed the world. You've changed my café, anyway.'

Because of me, Flat White now has a zero waste policy. Brendan recycles everything, even the coffee grounds. They go in the compost, which ends up in the flower boxes. He has banned plastic packaging. He only uses cups that can be recycled. Even the leftover food is recycled: at the end of the day, Brendan gathers up everything that hasn't been sold, and takes it to the homeless centre by the church.

I've also inspired the Murakamis. Because of Harry's spreadsheet, they saved 511 plastic items last month.

Mr Khan has been inspired too. He is planning to make Durdle Primary the greenest school in the whole country. He's banning plastic. He wants to fit solar panels on the roof, although apparently that's very expensive. He's going to ask the governors and the PTA to raise some money. I hope they do – it would be amazing!

Sparkle says I've inspired her, too. And Tariq and Claude. And William and Penelope. And Gareth and Muffin. And Mrs Ahmed and Mo and Joe. And all the other people who came on the

protest today, and all the people who saw our protest. Not to mention everyone who watched my interview.

All inspired by me.

So I should feel proud of myself.

Cheers!

There are some people I haven't inspired. Mr Schnitzel, for instance. The supermarket is using just as much plastic as before. I bet Mr Willow hasn't done anything, either.

But you can't win 'em all. That's what Dad says. He's right. I haven't saved the world. It's still in a mess. And my bogeys are still black. But I have done a few good things.

And doing something is definitely better than doing nothing.

Hope Jones' Blog

THURSDAY 6 FEBRUARY

Look!

Mr Crabbe has put out two wine bottles and a plastic yoghurt pot!

Obviously two bottles and a plastic pot isn't very much. But it's better than nothing, which is what has been in his recycling box every other week this year.

I would have liked to ring on his doorbell and say congratulations, but I didn't want him to call the police. So I just gave him a wave when I went past on my way to school.

He didn't wave back, but I don't mind. I'm just happy he put out his recycling.

Thanks for reading my blog. I hope you want to save the world too. Here are ten ways that you can help. Good luck! Love from Hope.

1. Always remember the three Rs.
   Reduce. Re-use. Recycle.

2. Try to use less plastic. It's difficult, I know. But why don't you try to use one less piece of plastic today? Just one. If we all used one less piece of plastic each day, imagine what a difference that would make!

3. Make a copy of Harry's spreadsheet. See how much plastic you can save.

4. Talk to the manager of your local shops and supermarkets. Ask what they are doing about the three Rs. How are they helping to reduce, re-use and recycle?

5. Talk to your friends and family about climate change. Discuss your hopes and fears for the future. What are they doing to help? How can we all change our behaviour and make a difference?

6. Write to a politician and ask them to take action on climate change.

7. Inform yourself. Educate yourself. Find out information about climate change. Learn about the people who have changed the world. I recommend reading about my heroes: Emmeline Pankhurst, Mahatma Gandhi and Nelson Mandela. Their lives are very inspiring. I have other heroes who are still alive and working today. For instance, I have been very inspired by Greta Thunberg, Ellen MacArthur and Kelsey Juliana. Why don't you find out more about them too? You will find lots of information about them on the internet.

8. Grow some of your own food. Plant some herbs, a packet of lettuce or cress, or some tomatoes. It will be delicious!

9. Pick up some rubbish. Discarded plastic ends up in the soil and the ocean. If you're on the beach or in the park, pick up a few pieces of plastic rubbish, and dispose of them responsibly.

10. Go outside. Go for a walk. Look at the trees. Climb a hill. Our planet is beautiful. Remember why we care about it. Remember what we are fighting for.